The
Put-Em-Rights

Enid Blyton

The Put-Em-Rights

AWARD PUBLICATIONS LIMITED

For further information on Enid Blyton please visit *www.blyton.com*

ISBN 978-1-84135-649-5

Illustrated by Chris Rothero
Cover illustration by Leo Hartas

First published 1947 by Lutterworth Press
First published by Award Publications Limited 1999
This edition first published 2010

Published by Award Publications Limited,
The Old Riding School, The Welbeck Estate,
Worksop, Nottinghamshire, S80 3LR

10 1

Printed in the United Kingdom

Contents

1

Summer Holidays Begin

It was the beginning of the summer holidays but Sally Wilson did not feel as pleased as all the other children of Under-Ridge Village. She put down her schoolbag, went to the window of her little bedroom, and looked out.

Sally loved school. She loved the daily company of the other girls, she enjoyed the bustle and excitement of school, she liked being top of her form and captain of the tennis team. She liked running the Nature Walks and the Debating Society. At school she was Somebody. At home in Under-Ridge Village, she was nobody. Her mother was the head of the little village school and she and Sally lived in the school house together. Her mother was a busy woman, keen on the little school, and, like Sally, always running this, that and the other.

Sally leaned her chin on her hand and looked over the fields to where a big grey house stood. It was the Rectory.

I wonder if Micky and Amanda are home, she

thought. I might walk over there today and see.

Micky and Amanda were the children of the Rector and his wife. Sally knew them quite well, for they went to the same church and attended the same Sunday classes. She liked Micky, with his dark wavy hair and deep blue eyes. She liked Amanda too. She had often been to tea with them.

I wish we could make life in Under-Ridge a bit more exciting in the holidays, thought Sally. It always seems so dull after school life. There doesn't seem anything to run, anything to organise, anything to get interested in. It's no good helping Mummy in all the things she does. She does them very well by herself, and she doesn't want me butting in.

This was quite true. Sally's mother loved running her different societies and guilds and institutes, but she liked running them by herself. She and Sally were very much alike – quick-brained, efficient, rather impatient people, who liked being the head of things.

'Sally,' her mother called up the stairs. 'Whatever are you doing, mooning up there? Come along down and show me your report.'

'I'm not mooning,' Sally called back impatiently, 'you know I never moon. I'm coming.'

She ran downstairs, looking a little sulky. She

gave her mother her school report. Mrs Wilson
slit it open and read it.

It was, as usual, excellent, but a remark at the
end annoyed Sally.

'Sally has run her class with her usual efficiency
and smoothness,' ran the report, 'but she must
not think that organising is everything. Kindness
and friendliness help the wheels to go round,
and there is a danger that Sally may forget this
in her zeal for perfection.'

'What a silly thing to say!' said Sally, indignantly. 'What does the Head mean by that? I'm
always kind and friendly to everyone.'

'Well, I suppose you put the class before the
girls,' said her mother. 'I mean – you wanted
your class to be so efficient that you perhaps

forgot that all the girls might not want to be just what you chose them to be.'

'It's mean of the Head to put in a remark like that,' said Sally, resentfully. She did not like to be found fault with, for she had a very good opinion of herself.

'There's a meeting on the village green tomorrow night,' said Mrs Wilson, changing the subject and slipping the report back into its envelope. 'There's a speaker coming to talk to children. It's the Tramping Preacher.'

'Oh, I've heard of him,' said Sally, interested. 'He goes all over the country talking to children, doesn't he, Mummy? He doesn't bother about grown-ups, he just goes to the children.'

'Yes, and I hear that he is starting all kinds of little societies up and down the country,' said Mrs Wilson. 'Run by children, of course. Maybe you could start one here, Sally, and run it. It would be something for you to do in the holidays.'

'I'll walk across to the Rectory and see if Micky and Amanda are going,' said Sally, 'I expect they are. Maybe the Tramping Preacher will be having a meal with them, and they can talk to him properly. I wish I could too.'

She left the house and set off down the lane, over a stile, and across the cornfields that led to the Rectory. The corn was green and high and made a whispering sound as Sally walked beside it. But she did not hear it, nor did she see the bright flash of the scarlet poppies in the corn. She was busy wondering whether she *could* start some sort of society that summer.

As soon as she came in sight of the Rectory she knew that Micky and Amanda were there for she heard cheerful voices and laughter. It sounded as if there were more than two people: Micky and Amanda must have visitors. Sally was not at all shy. She did not mind walking in, even if Micky had friends there. 'Hello!' she called as she came out on to the lawn and saw four children there. 'I haven't seen you for ages, Micky.'

Micky was a sturdy, good-looking boy of about twelve. Amanda, his sister, was eleven and as big as he was, very pretty, with charming ways. She was not very fond of Sally and often called her 'bossy' to herself.

The two other children turned and stared at Sally. One was a big boy of about thirteen with a merry smile, his hair rumpled over his brown forehead and his blue shirt open to show an equally brown neck. He was well dressed but untidy. By him was a much smaller girl of about ten, looking shy. She had a sweet face, a beautiful dress and large, rather scared-looking eyes. Like a rabbit about to run, thought Sally, as she went over the grass.

'Hello, Sally!' said Micky and Amanda. 'Can you stay and play? These are two friends of ours, Podge and Yolande. They're cousins, and they live at Four Towers. Podge's father has just bought it.'

Four Towers was the biggest house in Under-Ridge. It had a very large garden, which was kept by four gardeners, and a great number of glasshouses. Sally looked with respect at Podge. How rich his father must be!

'I wondered who had bought Four Towers,' said Sally, 'because I saw workmen there some time ago. When did you move in?'

'Yesterday,' said Podge. 'And Micky's mother, who is a great friend of my mother, invited us here for meals till we were settled in. What's your name?'

'Sally Wilson,' said Sally. 'Yours isn't really Podge, is it?'

'No. It's Claude Paget, and my cousin is Yolande Paget,' answered Podge. 'But Claude is such an awful name, so everyone calls me Podge, because I'm a bit fat.' He grinned lazily and Sally laughed.

She turned to Micky and Amanda. 'I really came over to see if you were going to the meeting on the village green tomorrow night,' she said. 'I hear the Tramping Preacher is coming.'

'Yes,' said Micky. 'He's coming to tea with us

before the meeting, and coming back to supper afterwards. Like to come to tea and supper too, Sally? You'll like the Preacher, he's great. I've heard him before. I warn you – he'll stir you up properly and make you do all kinds of things you never thought of doing before!'

Sally laughed scornfully. 'I'm not as easily stirred as all that,' she said. 'All the same, I'd like to hear him. Yes, I'd love to come to tea and supper. Are Podge and Yolande coming too?'

'They've got to go to the meeting with us,' said Micky, 'so they will be here for meals too. We can all go together. The village children will be going too, I expect. I bet your mother has rounded them all up and commanded them to go!'

Sally smiled. The village children were very much in awe of Sally's mother, their head teacher. If she said they were to go here, there or anywhere, they went. It never once occurred to Mrs Wilson that anyone would disobey her.

'Let's have a game,' said Podge. 'What about tennis? Can you play, Sally?'

'Yes, but my racket is at home,' said Sally.

'You can have mine,' said Yolande, terrified of playing with the bigger children. She handed it to Sally, who was pleased at being able to have a good game. She was easily the best. She was even better than Podge, who could have been very good if he had tried. Amanda too had the makings of a very good player, but she was too lazy to run for short balls. Micky yelled at her impatiently but nothing would hurry Amanda.

'You always play for yourself, not for your partner,' complained Micky, when Podge and Sally had beaten them well. 'You simply won't bother yourself to rush for a ball: you made me do all the running. You're lazy.'

'I know,' said Amanda, with a smile that showed a dimple, 'but I like to be lazy. It's nice to see other people rushing about all the time – but I'm not made that way. I don't like being on the go all the time like Sally, and I don't want to run this, that, and the other. I prefer to leave things to you others.'

They had to laugh at Amanda. She lay on her back on the grass grinning up at them, her shining golden hair round her face. 'Lazy little thing,' said Podge, digging her with his foot. 'Get up and have a race with me.'

'Good gracious, no! You race with Sally. She's always ready for anything and never gets tired. Do you, Sally?'

'No,' said Sally, who privately thought that tired people were lazy people. She could not understand anyone who loved doing nothing as much as Amanda did. She thought Amanda ought to help her mother more because there

14

was only one daily help in the big Rectory and a great deal to do. But Amanda's sweet-natured, hard-working mother did not nag at Amanda to help her, much as she would have liked her daughter to do so.

'I must get back,' Sally said, looking at her watch. 'I'll be along to tea tomorrow – and thanks awfully. I do hope we find plenty to do these holidays. It's so dull when there's nothing going on.'

'Oh dear!' said Amanda, watching Sally walking fast over the lawn. 'I think that's the beauty of holidays – having nothing to do! I'm glad I don't live with Sally. I should find her very tiring!'

2

The
Tramping Preacher

Sally walked over to the Rectory the next day at about four o'clock. The family were about to have tea in the garden and Micky and Podge were carrying out chairs.

'Hello!' called Micky. 'You're just in time. You can sit over here with Podge and Amanda.'

'I'll help bring out the chairs,' said Sally, who could not bear to sit down and see other people doing things: she just had to help. She was strong, and she helped to carry out a table, too.

'Well, Sally,' boomed the Rector's hearty voice behind her, 'helping as usual? You'll be as good a woman as that mother of yours one day! What we should do without her in this village I don't know!'

Many people said that about Sally's mother, and Sally was used to hearing it. She smiled and set down the table.

'Had a good report, Sally?' asked the Rector. 'But I needn't ask you that, I suppose. It's always excellent, isn't it? I only wish our lazy little

Amanda would get a better one. She has brains, but she doesn't use them.'

Amanda didn't mind being teased at all. She grinned at her father. She made no attempt to help with the chairs. There were plenty of people to do that!

A bell rang loudly in the house. 'That's the Tramping Preacher,' Amanda called out. 'He's walked all the way from Tidding Village – seven miles! He must be as energetic as you, Sally!'

Mrs Gray, the Rector's wife, came out into the garden with the visitor. The children stared at him, fascinated. He was burned a very dark brown, his eyes were intensely blue, and his thick shock of hair was black, streaked with grey. He wore corduroy trousers and a blue shirt, with a fairly respectable jacket over it.

'Here is the Tramping Preacher,' said Mrs Gray. The Rector shook hands. Then the Preacher turned to the watching children, and his piercing blue eyes burned into theirs. They fell under his spell at once.

There was no doubt about it; the Preacher had a way with children. Boys and girls, big and small, could not help listening to him, watching him, hanging on to his every word. He had a quiet, resonant voice, very pleasant to hear, and he spoke in simple, direct language that even the smallest child could understand. He was somehow a most exciting, unusual person.

'I feel as if he's awfully powerful,' whispered Yolande to Podge. 'You know, as if he might do miracles suddenly or something.'

Podge nodded. Big boy though he was, he too felt the strange, compelling power of the wandering preacher. The man was talking to the Rector and his wife, ignoring the children for the moment. Their turn would come later on the village green – then he would turn his piercing eyes on them, and pour his quiet, simple words into their ears.

The Rector was talking about his work with the children. 'You never preach to us grown-ups!' he said, laughing. 'Aren't we worth it, Preacher?'

The Preacher shook his head, smiling. 'I can't make a better world out of men and women,' he said, taking a piece of bread and butter in a thin brown hand. 'They're hard to change. But the children can make a better world if they start out right. The children don't know what power they have for good or evil. I tell them. And they listen to what I tell them.'

For one moment he flashed his deep blue eyes round the listening children and they felt his glance like a burning flame. Yolande glowed with sudden admiration for him. He was a wonderful man. She would do anything in the world for him! The children were too overawed to talk. Even Sally found nothing to say, although usually she had plenty. The Preacher talked of his work and of the various societies and bands that children in different places had started, and of the good work they had done. He thought the world of children. He believed in their goodness and strength and, in a most miraculous way, or so it seemed to the Rector, goodness and strength seemed to flow out of any children he preached to. The Rector wished he had the same power.

Tea was finished at last. Mrs Gray took the Preacher round the garden, while the children cleared away and got themselves clean and tidy for the meeting. They walked down to the green with the Preacher. The Rector and his wife went too, though the Preacher did not encourage grown-ups to attend his meetings: it was only the children he wanted. But the Rector thought he might learn something from the Tramping Preacher which would help him to handle some of the unruly children in his own village.

All the village children were there, sitting quietly on the green, under the eyes of Sally's mother. They rose when the Preacher came down the High Street. Some of the bigger boys looked sulky. They had wanted to play cricket, not to listen to a preacher. But in two minutes

the Preacher had them all under his spell in his usual easy way. There was not a sound to be heard as he talked. He told them stories. He made them laugh, and he made the tears start in their eyes. He stirred their hearts and their imaginations; he made them feel that they were strong and could do anything, anything!

The Preacher was a real spellbinder. He spoke for half an hour and it was much too short for the children. But the Preacher did not believe in overdoing things. He said goodbye, after telling the children he would be back some day to see how they were getting on. He said he felt sure the children of Under-Ridge would help the world along, and when he came back, he would like to hear how they had done it. He left the little gathering and went striding back to the Rectory over the fields, the Rector at his side. The children all sat quietly for a minute or two, thinking over the stirring message. They would do something, they really would! They would be better themselves, for one thing – and how they would help the grown-ups! Grown-ups needed helping. The Preacher had said so.

The five children who had come from the Rectory were very much moved, too. They walked a little way home and then sat down. 'Wasn't he marvellous?' said Amanda. 'I couldn't help feeling that I loved him, somehow.'

The others knew what she meant. The Preacher had a strange power. 'Shall we – shall we do what he said – and try to make the world a better place?' said Yolande in a small and rather timid voice.

'I think we ought to,' said Sally at once. 'And

what's more, we ought to do it properly. Make a real band of ourselves, and make rules and promises.'

'Oh, no rules,' said Amanda.

'Yes, rules,' Sally said firmly. 'Rules we've got to keep, too. It's no good beginning anything of this kind unless we do it properly.'

'You always want to do everything so very properly,' groaned Amanda. 'I like to be more easy-going.'

'Easy-going people never get anywhere worthwhile,' said Sally, rather primly. 'Look here – this is a wonderful chance for us all really to *do* something – to put wrong things right – to run our own village and help everybody.'

'What sort of wrong things do you mean to put right?' asked Micky.

'Oh – if we hear of anyone being cruel to anyone or anything we'll put it right,' said Sally. 'Or maybe we shall hear of someone having very bad luck. We can put that right, too, perhaps. We might try and teach Old Dicko not to steal, too – and try to get Mrs Lundy to be a bit cleaner.'

'Gracious! We'd never do that!' said Amanda. 'Mummy's tried for years.'

'Oh well, I don't say we *can* do these things,' Sally said. 'I'm only just saying they're the kind of things we might tackle. We mustn't shirk things because they seem hard or impossible.'

Podge had been very much stirred by the Preacher's talk too. He was a careless, rather arrogant boy who had rich parents and an easy life, but sometimes he yearned to do something worthwhile. He glanced at his little cousin Yolande. Her eyes were shining. She would like nothing better than to help, and with her sweet nature she would make a very good member of any band they formed.

'Well, let's start a little band or society, or whatever you like to call it, of our own,' Podge said. 'It may be a failure but at least we shall have tried. What do you think, Micky?'

'I'd like to,' Micky said at once. 'Dad and Mum would like us to, too. Let's all belong.'

Suddenly a voice came through the hedge, making them jump. 'Could I belong too? I want to help as well.'

The children turned. 'It's Bobby Jones!' said Amanda. 'I saw you at the meeting, Bobby.'

'Yes. Wasn't the Preacher great?' said Bobby, crawling through the hedge to join them. He was twelve years old, smooth-haired, with a pale, polite-looking face, and neat but old clothes. He lived with his mother, a widow, who was very poor but proud. Bobby went to the village school, but his mother was always telling him that he was much better than the other boys

there, and only went there because she could not afford anywhere else. So Bobby turned up his nose at his schoolfellows, and was always trying to make friends with the Rectory children. Amanda didn't mind him and found him useful in many ways, but Micky was bored with him.

'I think it's an awfully good idea to make a band of our own,' said Bobby. 'I thought of that myself and I was just wondering if I should ask you to join my band when I heard you talking about one yourselves. So I thought you wouldn't mind if I asked to join yours.'

Nobody particularly wanted Bobby to join, but it seemed rather mean not to let him when he had just said he was going to ask them to join his band.

There was a pause. Then Sally spoke. 'We haven't really made up our minds about our band yet. We'll have to do it properly – with rules and all that sort of thing.'

'That's a very good idea,' said Bobby, his eyes looking admiringly at Sally. 'You're so good at that kind of thing, aren't you, Sally? You'll be head of the band, of course.'

Sally felt she would like that very much, so she beamed at Bobby, making up her mind at once that he should belong straightaway.

'Oh, I don't know about that,' she said. 'Perhaps Amanda or one of the boys would like to be.'

'Not me!' said Amanda at once. 'Too much trouble. But why have we got to have someone at the head?'

'Well, it's better if there is someone to see to things properly,' said Sally, who liked to have everything just so. 'Let's meet here again tomorrow night, after thinking over everything carefully. We'll have all kinds of suggestions then. Hadn't we better go back to the Rectory now? It's almost suppertime.'

3

The Band of the Put-Em-Rights

The children told the Preacher that evening at supper that they were going to start a band of their own. He looked at the serious faces and seemed pleased. Already he knew he had thousands of children working for him, carrying out his ideas, trying to make the world a better place for everyone.

'Well, I wish you good luck,' said the Preacher when he left. 'I'll be back again, I hope, and then you shall tell me how you've all got on. Watch and pray and work – those are the things to do.'

That night in bed many children of the village thought about the blue-eyed preacher and his message for children. Six of them especially thought very deeply, for they were going to form a band. The Preacher had said that it wouldn't do just to say you wanted to help to conquer wrong in the world, you had to do things as well. It was Deeds, not Words, that counted.

Bobby Jones lay in his narrow bed and felt

pleased. If the other children kept their word and let him belong to their band, how proud he would be! He would be friends with the children from Four Towers then. Maybe he would be asked there to tea. How he could boast about that to the village children! 'My friend, Claude Paget of Four Towers.' That sounded very grand.

He wished Sally wasn't going to be in the band. It was true that he had suggested her being head of it, but he had only said that because he wanted to please her and to make her say he could belong, too. Sally was bossy, she ordered people about so much. Still, never mind, it would be marvellous to belong to such a splendid society or gang or band, whatever they were going to call it.

All the children were at the meeting-place the next evening, as arranged. Sally had a notebook in which she had written down her suggestions. No one else had written down anything.

'Well, here we all are,' said Sally, looking round. 'Now first of all – what shall we call our band?'

Nobody knew. But Sally had several suggestions. 'What about the Band of Service?' she said.

'*Awful!*' said Podge at once. 'How could you think of such a name?'

'It's not bad,' said Bobby, anxious to please Sally.

'It's – it's so sort of *ordinary*,' Amanda said.

'Well, *you* think of something then,' said Sally, rather cross.

'The Little Preachers,' said Amanda after a pause. Micky laughed.

'Quite good, only we don't preach.'

Sally looked at her list again. 'What about Ministering Children?' she said.

'You got that from the old book in Mum's bookcase,' said Micky at once. 'Didn't you?'

'Yes, I did. And I read the book, and I think

we're setting out to be ministering children,' said Sally, sticking up for herself.

'Well, the idea's right, but I simply *won't* be called a Ministering Child,' said Micky. 'I'd rather not be in the band. Much rather.'

'It's frightful,' said Podge. 'Wouldn't we be laughed at? Ministering Children! What you need is a sense of humour, Sally. How could you suggest a name like that?'

This time Sally was really offended. She shut her notebook with a snap. 'Very well,' she said, her rather tight lips getting tighter. 'I won't make any more suggestions. Perhaps you can make a really good one, Claude Paget.'

'Gracious – she must be cross to call me that!' said Podge, good-temperedly. He lay back on the grass and looked up at the blue July sky. 'Well, let's call ourselves something short and sensible. What about – the Put-Em-Rights?'

The others stared at him. Amanda broke into a peal of laughter. The Put-Em-Rights! How like Podge to think of a silly name like that! But it did just describe the band after all. Put-Em-Right – well, weren't they going to try to put wrong things right?

'I think it's marvellous!' said Amanda at once. Micky grinned too.

'So do I. I'd rather a hundred times be a Put-Em-Right than a Ministering Child.'

Yolande didn't mind which she was, but if the others liked Put-Em-Rights, well, she liked it too.

Bobby, seeing that everyone appeared to be voting for Podge's choice, added his word too. 'A jolly good name for us,' he said. 'Don't you think so, Sally?'

'No, I don't,' answered Sally. 'I think it's silly; it puts the whole thing on a lower plane, somehow.'

'It doesn't,' said Podge. 'It makes it more sensible, that's all.'

'Well, if you all like the name I must agree to it too,' said Sally, opening her notebook again. 'We will call ourselves "The Put-Em-Rights". My goodness, it does look silly, written down.'

'Let it,' grinned Podge. 'Better than us looking silly being called Little Preachers or Ministering Children. What about the rules, now?'

'I'm coming to that,' said Sally. 'I think our motto and chief rule should be what the Preacher himself said to us just before he went.'

'Watch – pray – and work,' said Amanda. 'Yes, that would be good.'

'We can watch out for things to put right – and pray about them – and then work to set them right,' Yolande said. 'The watching and praying part won't be difficult, but the other will.'

'We shan't mind difficulties,' said Podge. 'That will make it more fun.'

'Fun?' said Sally, raising her eyebrows. 'This is going to be serious work, Podge.'

'For goodness' sake, don't spoil it all by getting pious and preachy and solemn,' cried Podge, annoyed. 'I tell you, it will be *fun* to do this if we do it properly. But it won't if we go all prim and priggish.'

Sally flushed and frowned. Amanda made the peace.

'It won't help things along if we get cross with one another,' she said, slipping her arm through Sally's. 'Come on, let's get on with it. We've got two things settled, our name and our motto. Now for the rules.'

'We must all watch out and report to the Put-Em-Rights whenever we see anything wrong,' said Micky.

'Yes,' said Sally, and wrote it down.

'Then we must hold a meeting and decide how to put it right,' said Bobby. 'Everything must be discussed together. We mustn't decide things on our own.'

'That's a good rule,' Podge agreed. 'The whole band must bear the responsibility. Write it down, Sally.'

'And we must each take it in turn to put the things right,' said Sally. 'We can't all go off and tackle somebody – though there may be times when we'll all have to pull together at something.'

'Oh,' sighed Yolande, startled to find that she might have to do something difficult on her own. 'Oh, Sally, I couldn't possibly keep that rule. I'd never be able to do anything properly on my own. I'm not old enough.'

'Well, don't you want to belong, then?' demanded Sally. 'Shall I cross your name out, if you don't feel old enough?'

'She's old enough!' said Podge, putting his arm round the scared Yolande. 'Of course she can do things by herself – anyway, I shan't mind helping her, even if it isn't my turn.'

The small Yolande smiled gratefully at her big cousin. She was not a very brave little person. All the same, she couldn't bear the idea of being left out of the band now.

'We may find that we have to do difficult and awkward and unpleasant things,' said Sally, shutting her notebook. 'But we mustn't shirk anything at all. Wherever we find wrong, we must put it right.'

Now that the band was formed and they had a name, everyone was very eager to begin work. But how were they to begin? There didn't really seem anything they could straightaway set to work to put right.

'We'll all keep a watch out now,' Sally said, getting up. 'And if anyone has anything to report, they must call a meeting of the Put-Em-Rights at once. I say – what about a badge of some sort? It would be nice to have a button or something.'

'I'll make six,' Yolande said eagerly. 'Or perhaps Amanda could make half and I'll make half. They would be done quickly then. I've got some buttons at home I can cover. I'll embroider the three letters P E R on the buttons, and sew a tiny pin at the back. Then we can each wear one.'

Podge was not very thrilled about this, but the others thought it a good idea. 'And we won't tell a soul what P E R means,' said Amanda. 'We'll keep it a secret. Yes, I'll help you, Yolande. You bring the stuff in to me now, if you like. Or shall I come with you and make the badges at your home?'

'You come with me,' said Yolande. So Amanda, Micky and Podge got up to go back to Four Towers with Yolande. Sally followed too and, after a moment's hesitation, Bobby went with them. He hadn't been asked to go but he didn't think the others would tell him not to. And how thrilled his mother would be to know he had actually been to Four Towers! Yolande disappeared indoors with Amanda and Sally.

Podge, not knowing quite what to do with Bobby, let him wander round with Micky and himself. Bobby's eyes nearly fell out of his head when he saw the beautiful garden, the ripening fruit on the trees, the well-kept greenhouses. My, what tales he would have to tell his school-fellows now!

Upstairs, Yolande got out the buttons and little pieces of green material to cover them. Sally set to work to write out the rules of the band in her best handwriting. Amanda settled down to help Yolande make the badges but she soon tired of it and went to the window. She looked

down into the garden and saw the boys playing with the dogs. 'I'll be back in a minute,' she said, and disappeared. She didn't come back, so Yolande worked valiantly on by herself.

'Jolly mean of Amanda to leave you to do them all yourself after she said she'd help,' said Sally. 'Gosh, it's late. I must go. Shall I tell Amanda to come back and do her bit, Yolande?'

But it was too late. Amanda and Micky had to go too. 'What a shame there wasn't time to come back and help you, Yo,' said Amanda, appearing in the room to say goodbye.

'You mean you were too jolly lazy to sit and help,' said Podge, giving her a push. 'Now poor old Yolande will sit up and finish the lot. You *are* doing the badges beautifully, Yo!'

4

The First Wrong
turns Up

The six Put-Em-Rights wore their badges, all of
them but Podge feeling rather proud of them.
Podge thought himself too big to wear a silly
little button made by Yolande, but he was a
kind-hearted boy and did not like to hurt his
little cousin by not wearing it. They did not tell
anyone what the letters P E R meant. 'If we go
about telling everyone, we shall find it difficult
to put things right when we have to,' Sally said.
'People may not like to think that the Put-Em-
Rights are dealing with them.'

For a few days it seemed as if nothing was
wrong in the village. Podge wondered if he
should have a few words with the village policeman, and try to find out from him if there were
any poachers, burglars or people like that to deal
with. But on the whole he thought the policeman would probably deal with that kind of
people better than he could.

Then the first wrong turned up. It was Sally
who saw it and reported it. She was going along

by the river when she heard a dog yelping piteously, and her heart jumped for it was a very loud and terrified yelp.

The noise came from a cottage garden. The cottage belonged to a surly fellow called Fellin, who went out doing odd jobs as a gardener. Sally, pricking her ears up as she remembered she was one of the Put-Em-Rights, walked cautiously to the fence that ran at the end of the cottage garden.

She saw Fellin hitting a dog unmercifully. He had a big stick in his hand and he held the dog by the scruff of its neck. Sally trembled. She was just about to call out when the man threw down the stick, sent the dog rolling over and over, and disappeared indoors.

A woman in the next cottage saw Sally at the end of the two gardens and she called to her. 'Brute, isn't he? He hits that dog every day of his life. He ought to be reported, so he ought, the brute! He'll kill it one day!'

The dog crawled into the house after the man. It was a poor, mangy, thin creature, not at all beautiful. Its tail was too long and its ears were bitten. Sally waited till it had gone and then, as there were no more sounds of yelping, she hurried to the Rectory.

Micky, Amanda, Podge and Yolande were all there. Bobby Jones was the only member of the band who was absent. The others saw Sally's hot, excited face, and called to her. 'What's up? Anything happened?'

'I want to call a meeting of the Put-Em-Rights,' said Sally at once. 'We'll have to get Bobby too.'

'I'll go for him,' said Yolande, and she ran down the garden and into the lane where Bobby lived.

'Bobby!' she called, seeing him in the little garden there. 'Bobby! We're calling a meeting. You've got to come.'

Bobby felt proud. He spoke to the boy with him. 'I'll have to go to the Rectory. The others want me – you know, the band I belong to. You'd better go home and not wait for me.'

The boy nodded and watched Bobby go off with Yolande. Bobby wanted to know what the meeting was about, but Yolande didn't know.

'It's something Sally saw,' she said. 'She was all red and upset.'

Soon the six of them were sitting on the little lawn well away from the house, where they could talk without interruption.

'Come on, Sally – what's the matter?' said Podge, rather impatient at all the ceremony.

'Well,' Sally explained, 'I've seen a horrid wrong this morning, really horrid.' She told them of the poor miserable dog, half starved and beaten so cruelly.

'And the woman in the cottage next to Fellin's said he does that every day of his life!' finished Sally, indignantly. 'Don't you think that somehow we ought to put this right?'

Everyone agreed at once. They were all fond of animals, and Micky and Amanda had been heartbroken when Bengy, their old spaniel, had died that year. Something must certainly be done for the wretched little dog belonging to Fellin.

'Yes, this is the first thing we must tackle,' said Micky. 'Cruelty is terrible. Fellin must be a very wicked man. I'd no idea he was like that. He doesn't look too bad. He comes to help in the garden sometimes, and though he never has

40

much to say, I never thought he was so cruel. We must make inquiries about him and see what we can do for the dog.'

'How shall we decide whose job this is?' asked Podge. 'You know we said we must take it in turns to tackle things that turned up. We can't all plunge into it.'

'No. Too many cooks spoil the broth,' said Bobby agreeing, but hoping heartily that he would not have to put this wrong right. He was afraid of the sour-looking Fellin.

'We'll have to draw for it,' said Sally efficiently. 'I'll tear out a page from my notebook, cut it into six strips, write down our names, and put them into a hat. Then one of us can draw out a name, and whosever name it is must do the job.'

'But if it was my name, I couldn't possibly!' Yolande said, looking really scared.

'You joined this band and you've got to do your bit,' said Sally. 'You can pray harder than ever if it's you, and I expect you'd think of some way to do it.'

This was not very comforting, but Yolande did not like to say any more. 'Please, God, don't let it be me!' she said secretly over and over again as she watched Sally cutting up six strips of paper.

The names were written on them. Nobody

had a hat so Amanda fetched a flowerpot. The strips were put into it and well shaken.

'Yolande, you're the youngest. You can draw,' said Sally. 'Shut your eyes.'

With a trembling hand and still muttering her fervent prayer, Yolande felt about among the strips. Which was her own? If only she knew, then she wouldn't draw it! But that would be cheating. So it was just as well she didn't know or, dreadful thought, she might have cheated! The little girl pulled out a strip and then did not dare to open her eyes and look at it.

'Whose name is it, silly?' said Sally impatiently, half hoping it was her own, for she was feeling very efficient and thorough at that moment. She snatched the paper from Yolande and read the name.

'Micky! It's you. You're the first Put-Em-Right to tackle anything.'

'Oh,' said Micky, rather taken aback. 'Gosh! What do I do?'

The Put-Em-Rights settled down to a discussion. Yolande felt so relieved that the name was not hers that she had just as much to say as the others.

'It's no good giving the man a talking-to, I'm sure,' said Sally, much as she believed in 'talkings-to' and 'dressings-down'. 'You'll have to go about it some other way, Micky.'

'Yes, perhaps you could make the man think that the dog was a very nice dog who would be grateful for kindness, or something like that,' said Yolande.

Podge looked at her. 'I rather think that's the best line to go on,' he agreed. 'Quite a good idea, Yo.' Yo went red with pleasure.

'It would be better than reporting the man to the RSPCA,' said Sally. 'We can always tell the Prevention of Cruelty to Animals people if we can't make the man see reason. But all that would do would be to rescue the dog without helping the man.'

'Yes; if we could make the man kind, as well as making the dog happy, that would be a really worthwhile thing to do,' said Amanda. 'We'd be helping both. Daddy always says that anyone who is cruel is to be pitied.'

Micky scratched his head and frowned. 'Well, I don't feel as if I pity Fellin nearly as much as I pity his dog. And it's going to be jolly difficult to change old Fellin, let me tell you. He hasn't got that mean, sour look on his face for nothing!'

'It's good to have something difficult to tackle,' Sally said brightly.

'You sound jolly priggish,' said Micky. 'You wait till your turn comes! All right, all right. I'm not grumbling because I've got to do something first. I said I'd belong to the band and I'm proud to – but I don't want to make a mess of this. Exactly how do you propose I should tackle Fellin?'

'Well, he comes to work in your garden, doesn't he?' said Podge. 'Can't you get into conversation with him – and ask him about his dog – and tell him what a nice creature it is – and get in a bit about kindness to animals, and how nice it is to have dogs loving you, and all that?'

'I'll try,' said Micky, who didn't somehow feel that these words would work wonders with Fellin. 'Amanda, you must help me.'

'I'll come and hear what you say,' said Amanda. 'But you're jolly well not going to make me do the talking, Micky.'

'You wouldn't, even if I begged you to, lazy!' said Micky. 'I hope you get something most awfully difficult to do when your turn comes. You always wriggle out of everything if you can!'

'Now don't squabble, you two,' said Sally.

'All right, teacher,' said Amanda. Sally flushed. She hated being teased, and she didn't like being called 'teacher'. That was what all the village children called her mother.

'Fellin comes tomorrow, I think,' said Micky. 'I'll tackle him then.'

'I'll say a very big prayer for you, Micky,' said Yolande, 'so that things will go well and you'll be able to change Fellin and make sure the dog won't be miserable any more.'

'Good old Yo,' said Micky. 'I know jolly well

I can't do things all by myself. I'll do what I can tomorrow, but I may have to work on Fellin for a week or two before he comes round to our point of view. So don't expect me to do this all in a hurry. It's no good rushing things.'

'Right,' said Podge. 'And go on keeping your eyes open, everyone. Bobby, you talk to your mother, and you talk to yours, Sally, and you to yours, Amanda. They know everyone in the village and all that goes on, so you may hear something that the Put-Em-Rights can tackle. We don't want these hols to slip by without doing anything much.'

'There's probably quite a lot under our very noses that we could help in,' said Amanda. 'Well, anyway, good luck to our first Put-Em-Righter!'

'Good luck, Micky!' said everyone, and then the meeting broke up.

5

Micky
gets to Work

Bobby talked to his mother that night, and Sally and Amanda also talked to theirs. Podge and Yolande did not say anything to Podge's mother, for they both knew that she was not interested in the village people.

Bobby's mother was surprised at her son's sudden interest in the villagers but she was quite willing to talk about them. She looked down on them and kept herself aloof, and it was always a sore point with her that her precious Bobby had to mix with the village children so much.

'I'm so glad you are making such nice friends,' she said to Bobby. 'Your dear father would have been pleased. It's nice that you go to Four Towers so much too. Claude and Yolande are lovely children. I wish you had better clothes, Bobby – but I have so little money.'

Bobby wished he had nicer things too. His clothes were always so worn and old, and he grew out of them so quickly. The village children were better dressed than he was. Still, it was something to be able to lord it over them, talking of 'my friend, Claude Paget'.

'Go on!' the village boys said rudely. 'You and your Claudes! You just suck up to them. They don't think anything of you, really! You just push yourself in, and they're too polite to push you out!'

Bobby couldn't help feeling there was a lot of truth in this. He had pushed himself in. And he always felt that although the others were very polite to him, they were not really warm and friendly. He felt hurt about it.

Don't I always agree with them? he thought. Don't I praise them, and say 'yes, yes, yes,' all the time? I never disagree or argue like Podge or Micky.

If Bobby had but known it, the others would have liked him very much better if he had argued sometimes, or disagreed. As it was, they hardly paid any attention to him or to what he said, knowing that he would always agree – that he would never put forward any ideas of his own.

Bobby was foolish that night. He gave the secret of the band away to his mother, although he and all the others had promised to keep it to themselves. But Bobby could not resist boasting, even to his own mother.

'It's a deep secret, Mum,' he said, 'but perhaps you'd like to know that Claude and

Yolande Paget, and Micky and Amanda Gray, asked me to belong to a band they've got up – it's called the Put-Em-Rights.'

'What a peculiar name!' said his mother, surprised. 'Whatever are you going to put right?'

Bobby told her about the Tramping Preacher and everything. His mother did not care about the helping and putting-right idea, but she cared very much that her Bobby had actually been asked to join the band. She flushed with pleasure.

'That will be very nice for you, Bobby,' she said. 'I'm really glad you're making such nice friends. Does anyone else belong?'

'Sally Wilson does,' said Bobby. 'She's sort of head of it.'

'Oh, that Sally!' said his mother, who didn't like Sally at all and thought her interfering. 'She's going to be a regular busybody like her mother! Mrs Wilson is always on at me to do this, that, and the other. Says I don't mix enough. As if I want to mix with the village people here, and make jam at the Institute, and go over to Tidding Hospital to mess about there . . .'

'Well, Sally's in the band too,' Bobby said, knowing that if he didn't interrupt his mother would go on for a long time about Mrs Wilson. 'But I don't take much notice of her, Mum. I just put my own ideas forward and the others agree to them. I suppose *I* really run the band.'

His mother beamed. She thought that was wonderful.

'The thing is, Mum, as we've made this band to put things right where they are wrong, we've got to get to work,' said Bobby. 'I suppose you don't know anything in the village we could help to put right, do you?'

Mrs Jones could think of a great many things! She disapproved of a lot of people and their 'goings-on' in Under-Ridge. But most of them were impossible for children to tackle. She would like to have that conceited Mrs Brown told not to wear such fashionable clothes! She would like to make the tradespeople more polite – they were none of them as civil to her as they ought to be!

'Well,' she said at last, 'there's that dirty, untidy Mrs Potts. Why don't you tackle her, Bobby? She's a real disgrace to the village – and that baby of hers is always crying, and so dirty. It could be a nice little thing if it was clean and tidy. Her husband's away in the Navy, but what he'll say when he comes back and sees that nice little cottage so filthy, the garden all weeds, and the baby a dirty, squalling little creature, I don't know! Run away and leave her to it, I should think.'

Bobby thought that Mrs Potts and her dirty little baby would be a good job for the Put-Em-Rights to tackle, and he said so.

'You tell her she ought to be ashamed of herself!' said Mrs Jones. 'Bringing up that poor little baby of hers like that! You just tell her that.'

Bobby thought that the Put-Em-Rights would hardly go about the task in that way, but he didn't say so. He hoped it wouldn't fall to him to tackle it; he thought it was really a job for one of the girls.

Sally had a talk with her mother, too, but Mrs Wilson was busy and inattentive. 'Ask me another time, Sally,' she said. 'I'm busy now. I haven't time to discuss the village people with you. Go among them yourself if you want to find out about them, and make friends. Though you'll probably find, as I do, that they're very standoffish, and you can't get much out of them.'

Sally didn't mean to go and find out anything herself. She had already reported Fellin and his dog to the band. If her mother had had any ideas to offer, she would have told the band these, but Sally didn't like the villagers enough to go and talk with them. I've done my bit in reporting Fellin, she thought. I wonder how Micky will tackle that. He's not lazy like

Amanda, or don't-carish like Podge, so maybe he'll do the job quite well.

Amanda, too, had tried to find out from her mother if there was anything wrong in the village that could be put right. But Mrs Gray did not discuss the affairs of the villagers with anyone except the Rector, certainly not with her children. She held that if the villagers came to her for help, it was their own private affair, and no one else need be told about it. Therefore the villagers trusted her and came to her and the Rector for help in all kinds of matters.

So Amanda did not get any helpful information at all from her mother. However, she happened to overhear a remark that Alice, the daily help at the Rectory, made to her mother, which set her thinking.

'That poor little baby of Mrs Potts, it doesn't get on at all,' said Alice. 'Mrs Potts wants a good shake-up, it seems to me: lazy and dirty, she is, and her husband away and all!'

Ah! thought Amanda. Now that's something the Put-Em-Rights might do. I'll tell them tomorrow.

She told Micky that night and he agreed that Mrs Potts and the baby were their job. 'For the sake of the baby,' he said. 'Oh, Amanda, I hope I tackle Fellin all right. I don't want to make him any worse than he is already!'

'You won't,' Amanda said. 'Don't worry, Mick. We'll soon all be tackling different things, and we can't expect to get everything right at once. It may take weeks and weeks to do some things.'

Fellin came the next day. At his heels was the thin, half-starved little mongrel. Micky, looking out of the window, was delighted to see it.

'Look there,' he said to Amanda. 'Fellin has actually brought his dog with him. That will make things easier for me. You come along too, Mandy, and if you can put in a word to help, you must.'

After breakfast the two children went down to where Fellin was hoeing. The garden was too big for the Grays, who hadn't nearly enough money to keep a full-time gardener for it. So the Rector got odd-job men like Fellin to come and do urgent jobs from time to time. Most of the garden he and Mrs Gray did themselves, with occasional help from Micky, and very rare help from Amanda.

'Good morning, Mr Fellin,' said Micky.

'Morning,' said Fellin, ungraciously. 'Get to heel, Midge.'

Midge the dog crawled to Fellin's heels, his tail drawn between his legs. He lay there, perfectly still, his eyes fixed on Micky.

'What a nice dog!' said Micky brightly.

Fellin said nothing. 'He – he looks so intelligent,' went on Micky. 'I love dogs, don't you, Mr Fellin?'

'I like dogs that *are* dogs!' said Fellin, hoeing viciously at a patch of weeds. 'That there thing isn't a dog. It's just a bundle of trouble. Chasing hens and sheep and barking at night till all the neighbours complain. Many's the time I've thought to get rid of it.'

'But – but he looks such a dear little dog,' said Amanda, trying to help. 'He's got such nice eyes – and a nice black nose – and –'

Fellin looked at her in surprise. He was not used to hearing praise of his dirty, mangy little mongrel. He looked down at Midge to make sure it really was his dog they were talking about.

'It's so nice to have a dog for a friend, isn't it?' said Micky, trying again. 'I had a dog once – a spaniel called Bengy. But he died. He was the best dog in the world and went with me everywhere like a real friend.'

There was such feeling in Micky's voice that Fellin looked at him with interest. 'Ay,' he said, 'it must be good to have a dog like that. That's why I got Midge here, because I was lonely and wanted company. I thought maybe a dog would cheer me up a bit. But this one, he's a failure right enough. Gets me into no end of trouble he does, killing hens and things. I thrash him hard to stop him, but it's not a bit of good. He goes off and gets me into trouble again.'

'He looks awfully thin,' said Micky, looking at the wretched dog. 'Do you feed him enough?'

'He can pick up food for himself all right,' said Fellin. 'No call to spoil a dog, is there? Let him fend for himself, same as I do! He's a poor fellow, this dog, though; only half a dog, I say. No good to anyone. He was a nice little pup, though. I wasn't to know he'd grow into this ugly creature.'

'Don't hurt him so much,' Micky said earnestly. 'Try a little kindness instead.'

'Pah!' said Fellin, scornfully. 'What do you suppose kindness would do to a dog like that? Just make him worse than ever, see? He only understands a good whipping.'

Micky felt that he was not getting on very fast. He was racking his brains for something else to say when he heard his name called.

'Micky! Where are you?' It was Bobby Jones, looking rather important.

'I'm here,' said Micky. 'What do you want?'

'To call a meeting,' said Bobby. 'I've heard of something else.'

'Right,' said Micky, rather glad to have an excuse for leaving Fellin. 'Podge and Yolande will be here soon.'

'I called for Sally on my way up,' said Bobby. 'She's waiting over on the lawn.'

Micky bent down to pat Midge. The dog growled and tried to snap.

'What did I tell you?' said Fellin triumphantly. 'Kindness ain't no good to him! Spiteful little cur, he is. You give him a kick and he'll understand *that*!'

Micky and Amanda said nothing. They hurried off with Bobby. Micky secretly thought that Midge was as sour as his master!

6

Another Wrong to
put Right

Soon the six Put-Em-Rights were once more in deep discussion. Amanda was interested to hear that Bobby had brought the same case for reporting as she had heard about the night before.

'I was going to suggest that we should see what we could do about the Potts's baby,' she said.

'Great minds think alike,' said Bobby, feeling pleased that he and Amanda had had the same idea. 'Now – who'll tackle it? I think one of the girls had better try this. Boys aren't any good where babies are concerned.'

Yolande began to feel afraid again. Gracious, she would never be able to tackle Mrs Potts and the baby! She didn't like dirty babies either. They smelled – and Yolande always felt sick when there was a bad smell.

Amanda and Sally looked at one another. Sally felt that she wouldn't mind a bit if she had to tackle this job. She felt she could put Mrs Potts right and make her see to her baby properly without very much trouble. She just wants showing how, I expect, thought the efficient Sally.

'Yes,' she said aloud, 'perhaps it *is* a job for one of us girls. We'll draw for it.'

Once again poor Yolande had to go through the agony of drawing a slip, but mercifully she drew, not her own name, but Amanda's. Sally felt disappointed. Amanda didn't seem to mind being the chosen one. She was sure the others would help her! Amanda was clever at wriggling out of responsibility of all kinds. She never worried much about anything. She went through life in her own lazy way, quite happy.

'It's me,' she said, looking at the slip. 'Well – let's talk about it. What do I do?'

There was a long discussion. Sally was all for giving Mrs Potts a good talking-to, and Bobby politely agreed with her. But Podge shook his head.

'Do remember that grown-ups are grown-ups, and not even a lazy, easy-going person like Mrs Potts is likely to listen to priggish talk from children,' he said. Sally glared at the word 'priggish', which she felt sure Podge was directing at her and her alone. Podge grinned back.

'It's no good glaring, Sally. You may be awfully efficient and have a tidy mind yourself

and all that, but it's surprising how many people dislike that in others. I do myself.'

'I expect you do!' burst out Sally. 'You're so untidy and careless and don't-carish yourself that you can't understand me wanting to have things in good order. You're always losing things and spoiling things, aren't you?'

Sally's words were unpleasant but they were true. Podge, used to plenty of money and possessions, was very careless with both. Already in the first week of the holidays he had lost a new pocket-knife through leaving it carelessly on the bank where he had been sitting; he had lost his blazer; and he had left his bicycle out in the rain two nights running, so that it no longer looked brand-new.

'Shut up,' said Podge. 'I'm not going to be ticked off. They're not your things I lost!'

'I should think not!' said Sally, angered at being told to shut up. 'I take a bit more care of my things! The trouble with you is that you have too many things, and life is made too easy for you. You ought to have been born poor, like Bobby, then you'd have learned to value things more, and be responsible, and . . .'

Bobby didn't like being referred to as poor. He flushed and stood up.

'If we're all going to quarrel, we'd better put off the meeting till another time,' he said, and the others stared at him in surprise. They were not used to Bobby taking the lead at all. Podge was quickly ashamed of the quarrel, though he bitterly resented Sally's home truths. He knew he was careless; he knew he was irresponsible where his own things were concerned. But Sally wasn't going to be allowed to point these things out to him.

'We're idiots to squabble,' he said, his good-natured smile coming back. 'Sit down, Bobby. Let's change the subject. How is Amanda going to tackle Mrs Potts?'

'What about going about it in the same way that Micky was told to go about Fellin's dog?' Yolande said eagerly. 'You know – going to see Mrs Potts – and then praising her baby and say-ing how sweet she'd be if she was well-dressed and all that kind of thing!'

'I could do that all right,' agreed Amanda, who had often heard her mother saying things like this. 'It's what Mummy calls "suggestion". You put an idea into people's heads and they like it, and carry it out themselves.'

'Well, you go and put a suggestion into Mrs Potts's head,' said Micky. 'I hope you have more success than I had with Fellin. The more I suggested to him that Midge was a nice little dog, the more he seemed to think that he was an awful creature. My suggestion seemed to work the opposite way.'

Just as Micky spoke there came an awful howling that made them all jump violently.

'What is it?' Yolande said fearfully.

'It's that man beating his dog again,' said Sally, fiercely. She jumped up.

'Look out,' said Podge. 'It's Micky's show, this, not yours, Sally. Don't go and spoil everything for him.'

'No, I'll manage it if I can, Sally,' said Micky, and he went off in the direction of the howls.

The others followed at a distance. Micky rounded a corner and came upon Fellin thrashing the unfortunate dog again.

'You'll have my father out here in a minute,' said Micky, not being able to think of anything else to say. 'What's Midge been doing? Do stop!'

At the mention of the Rector Fellin dropped

the dog he was thrashing, and the creature at once crawled under a bush and lay there, whining softly.

'I reckon your pa would just about treat Midge the same, if he knew what he's been and gone and done,' growled Fellin, throwing his stick into a hedge. 'You look at that hen there!'

Micky looked. There was a hen crouching in terror nearby; half its feathers had gone and they were blowing about on the grass. It was quite plain that Midge had flown at the hen. 'Perhaps he was hungry,' suggested Micky. He looked at the dog. It certainly was an unpleasant-looking animal, cringing and cowering, its ribs showing clearly under its skin.

It looked up at Micky, the whites of its eyes showing. The boy felt sorry for it. 'I'll get it something to eat,' he said, and went off. He came back with a dog's bowl full of scraps and set it down by the dog. Midge crept out, his tail between his legs. In three gulps he had gobbled up the whole meal. It was plain that he was starved.

'Look at that,' said Micky, pityingly. 'He's hungry enough to eat the dish!'

Fellin went on with his hoeing and paid no more attention to the boy. Micky made affectionate noises to Midge and was rewarded by a thump of his tail. Just one thump and no more.

Then the tail went back between the dog's legs, making him look as if he had no tail at all.

The others, who were watching, went off on errands of their own. Micky stayed behind with Fellin and the dog. Perhaps if he could feed Midge up a bit, and brush his coat, and make him friendly and affectionate, Fellin would see how to treat animals properly, and would be kind to Midge. Then Micky would have done two things – made Midge happy, and helped to change the sour Fellin into somebody a little nicer. So Micky tried to make friends with Midge. Fellin went on working stolidly, remarking after a while in surprise that he wouldn't have thought a boy like Micky would have fussed over a mongrel like Midge.

'He's got the makings of a very nice little dog in him,' said Micky at once. 'He could be a good friend to you, I'm sure, Mr Fellin, if you were kinder to him.'

'There's some people and some creatures that gets on better with kicks,' said Fellin. 'And Midge is one of them.'

Micky sighed. It was very, very hard to put things right when people like Fellin and dogs like Midge had to be dealt with. He played with the idea of buying Midge a collar, for the dog had none.

Then he dismissed the idea from his mind. Collars cost money, and Micky was mean with his money. Amanda would spend generously on everyone at Christmas time, but Micky wouldn't. Amanda would empty her money-box and give her money away to anyone in trouble, but Micky thought two or three times about it before he did such a thing – and then he would never give away all he had.

No, he couldn't buy Midge a collar – that was certain. He had plenty of money in his money-box; but he wanted to buy himself a new bicycle if he could, and he needed every penny. It was even a nuisance when people's birthdays came along, because then he had to part with some of his money again.

Micky left Midge with Fellin and went back to find the others. He looked a little gloomy.

'Not getting on very well?' asked Podge. 'Well, Fellin is a hard nut to crack. Still, you may make friends with the dog, and that will be a good thing for Midge. It's a pity Fellin can't get anything out of the dog – he's just the man to want a bit of company and dog-love.'

'It would be almost as hard to love Midge as to love Fellin,' said Amanda. 'Well, if I know anything about old Mick, he won't give up. Will you, Micky?'

'Of course not,' said Micky. 'Fellin's going to work here for weeks – and I'm going to work on him and on Midge too! You bet!'

'Well, I'm off to Mrs Potts,' said Amanda, waving her hand to the others. 'She may not be quite so difficult as Fellin and Midge!'

7

Amanda tackles
Mrs Potts

Yolande went down to the village with Amanda.

'I won't interfere,' she assured her. 'I just want to see what you do and say. I'm terrified of when my turn comes; I hope it's last of all, then perhaps I shall have learned from you all, and I shall know what to do.'

'You're frightened of simply everything, Yo,' said Amanda. 'Of cows and bats and mice and going into a room full of people, and going to parties and all kinds of things.'

'I suppose I'm an awful coward,' Yolande said sadly. 'But I can't seem to help it. You know, I won a prize at school last term, Amanda – but at the prize-giving, when my name was called, I was too afraid to go up for my prize! Wasn't it awful?'

'Yes. Very silly of you,' said Amanda, who would have loved to go up to the platform for a prize, but had never yet worked hard enough to win one. 'Gosh, isn't it hot? Let's sit down and rest for a bit, shall we?'

'Well, wouldn't it be better to go to the village and get your job over?' asked Yolande, who knew that once Amanda sat down and began to talk, she might easily go no farther. Amanda was so lazy.

'Plenty of time for that,' said Amanda, and flung herself down in some cool, long grass. 'Isn't this weather heavenly? Look up at the blue sky, Yo. It seems to dissolve farther and farther away the harder you look at it.'

Yolande lay on her back too. The blue sky *was* funny to look at: you couldn't really see it when you looked hard at it. Then a cloud came over the sun and Yolande sat up.

'Come on,' she said to Amanda. 'It will be lunch-time before you get along to the village. You *are* lazy, Amanda. Sally would have been there and back by now.'

'Oh, don't talk about bossy Sally to me,' Amanda said lazily. 'She makes me tired! I think it would almost have been better to have let her do everything, not take it in turns!'

'Do get up,' said Yolande, but Amanda turned obstinate then, and wouldn't. Soon the church clock struck half past twelve, and Yolande felt cross. 'There! It's lunch-time. I'll have to go. You haven't done a thing, Amanda! I don't think you're a good member of the Put-Em-Rights at all!'

Amanda was ashamed then. She sat up, put her hands through her hair to smooth it, and frowned. 'Gracious! I'd no idea it was so late. I'll go this afternoon.'

Yolande sped off to Four Towers, thinking that Amanda was a real putter-off. Too much would be done if things were left to Sally – but far too little if things were left to Amanda!

And perhaps nothing at all if they were left to me! thought little Yolande, honestly. I'm really so scared of things. I wish I wasn't. I suppose I was born that way and I'll never be any different.

Micky was very scornful to Amanda when she came back and confessed she hadn't even got as far as the village. 'Just like you!' he said. 'Always wriggling out of doing things! You said you'd take it in turns to feed the goldfish and it was your turn today, and you didn't do it. I bet you'll never get as far as Mrs Potts's cottage!'

'Well, I will,' said Amanda. 'And don't you tell the others I didn't go this morning. I'll be back before tea.'

So, after her lunch, Amanda set out once more, this time without Yolande. She walked steadily to the village and came to Mrs Potts's cottage. It was a dirty place and the garden was full of weeds, with a few plants struggling to grow among them. One rose-tree stood in the middle, with a deep red rose on it. The curtains

68

at the windows were dirty. The front doorstep was unwashed. The brass handle of the little blue door was dull and unpolished. From the cottage came the wail of a baby.

Amanda walked up to the front door and knocked. In her hand she carried a parish magazine. This was her excuse for calling. She waited on the doorstep but no one came. Amanda knocked again. Still there was no answer, and not even a movement came from the house. But the baby wailed all the time. It was such a hopeless, pathetic wail that Amanda couldn't bear it. Surely the baby could not be alone in the house?

She pushed at the door, turning the handle. It opened, and Amanda found herself in a small, dark and smelly little sitting-room. At the back was an equally smelly kitchen. The baby was not in either of these places.

It must be upstairs, thought Amanda, and ran to see. Upstairs was one small bedroom, and another even smaller, not much bigger than a big cupboard. In the larger of the two rooms was the baby.

It had been put into a cot – and it must have fallen out! There it was on the floor, crying help-lessly. It was not more than nine months old, and could just crawl. 'Oh, you poor little thing!' cried Amanda, and ran to pick it up. It was a dirty baby and a smelly one. Its nose needed wiping, and its curls were damp with heat. Its clothes were filthy.

Amanda sat down on a chair and took the baby on her knee. She was passionately fond of her dolls at home and had often longed for them to come alive so that she might nurse them properly on her lap, feeling them warm and moving. She had never held a baby before, and it seemed to her like a lovely big doll come alive.

'Dear little thing!' she said, and looked down at its big dark eyes. The baby blinked at her. 'You open and shut your eyes properly,' said Amanda in delight. 'And you feel so warm and soft.' The baby, delighted at being picked up and talked to, recovered from its fright in falling out of its cot and suddenly smiled.

'*Oh!*' said Amanda, and lost her heart to the baby at once. It was a beautiful child, a little girl with black curly hair, dark eyes, curling eyelashes and tiny ears. But it was pale and did not look very healthy.

'It's a pity you're not clean and sweet, as babies ought to be,' said Amanda, seriously. 'You'd be lovely then. And you ought to have rosy cheeks, you know. But I don't wonder you haven't, if your mother leaves you alone in this smelly bedroom on a hot day like this.' Amanda rocked the baby to and fro. The little thing crowed and waved its hands about. It liked Amanda immensely.

Just then Amanda heard someone coming in at the door downstairs. Then she heard the door shut. Someone moved about the kitchen. Amanda felt a bit scared. Steps came up the stairs and a thin-faced young woman walked into the little bedroom. How she stared when she saw Amanda with the baby.

'Oh – Mrs Potts,' said Amanda, still hugging the baby, 'I heard your baby crying terribly and I came in, and the baby had fallen out of her cot. So I picked her up and comforted her. She's not hurt. I hope you don't mind.'

Mrs Potts looked at the pretty, neat little girl in the dirty bedroom. 'I suppose you've been snooping round and seeing how dirty and ragged everything is,' she said. 'Yes, I know what everyone says about me! Now you'll go back to the Rectory and tell everyone what a filthy place this is. I know you and your kind!'

'Oh!' said Amanda, shocked at the bitter words and tone. 'I wouldn't dream of saying nasty things, Mrs Potts. But why don't you keep everything clean? It's a sweet little cottage – and this is such a sweet little baby.'

Mrs Potts sat down wearily on a rickety chair and wiped her forehead with a handkerchief.

'I haven't got any money,' she said. 'What bit I have I go out and earn; and the places I go to won't have the baby because she cries a lot. It's her teeth, I suppose. I'm too tired when I come in to do anything much here except look after the baby. And anyway, I've got no money for soap and cloths and brushes and brooms. I know the village says I'm lazy, but I'm not. I don't feel well, that's what it is.'

Certainly Mrs Potts did not look very well.

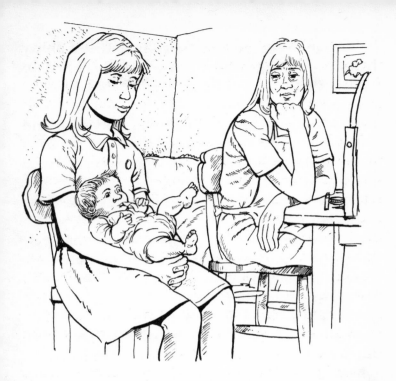

Amanda wondered about her husband. Didn't he pay her anything to buy things for herself and the baby?

'Won't your husband give you lots of money when he comes back?' said Amanda, hugging the baby. 'I expect he will.'

'He's been gone a year now, and for ten months I haven't heard a word, not even a post-card,' said young Mrs Potts. 'That's all he cares about me and the baby. He's never even seen Emily – that's the baby.'

'What a pretty name,' said Amanda, 'a pretty name for a pretty baby. If she was all dressed up and clean, Mrs Potts, she'd look simply beautiful.'

'Well – you bring me clothes and soap and I'll turn around and do this cottage and the baby too,' said Mrs Potts in a mocking voice. Amanda answered at once.

'All right, I will! You can make this place look really sweet.'

'I don't mean it,' said Mrs Potts wearily, getting up. 'I don't want to do anything these days. Stick the baby back into its cot. Your ma won't like you staying here so long.'

'Could I come and take the baby out sometimes – when you're at work?' said Amanda, putting the baby reluctantly back into its cot. 'I do love her. I really do. She's better than all my dolls.'

'You don't want to be seen wheeling out my broken-down old pram!' said Mrs Potts, in surprise.

'I don't mind how broken-down or old it is,' said Amanda. 'It's the baby I want. Do get her all nicely dressed for me to wheel out, Mrs Potts. I'll bring you soap and clothes, really I will.'

'I'll see,' said Mrs Potts. Amanda went down the steep little stairs, wrinkled up her nose at the dirty kitchen, and let herself out. She walked back to the Rectory, feeling rather pleased with herself.

All the others were there except Bobby. 'How did you get on?' said Micky eagerly. 'Did she turn you out?'

'Of course not,' answered Amanda, scornfully. 'I made friends with her. And I held the baby. And I'm going to take her some soap so that she can clean up her cottage and wash the baby's clothes. And I'd like to take her some nice baby clothes too. I've told her I'd like to take the baby out for walks sometimes, when she's out working. She has to leave the baby behind then, poor thing. It had tumbled out of its cot today.'

The others gazed at Amanda admiringly. She certainly seemed to have done quite a lot. 'I'll ask Mum if she's got any old baby clothes,' said Podge.

'And we'll buy some soap,' said Sally. 'We'll each give some money towards it.'

Micky didn't want to give up money to buy soap. 'Oh, we'll ask Mother to give us some,' he said.

'No,' said Sally firmly. 'This is our own affair, the affair of the P E R's. We'll buy the soap ourselves.'

So Micky had to give some money with the others, though he didn't like it. Bobby didn't like it either, for he had very, very little money. He did not like to say so, although if he had mentioned that he couldn't afford it, the others would have agreed at once. But none of them realised quite how poor Bobby's mother was.

Podge's mother found some old baby clothes she was going to give away and, with much amusement, handed them to Podge. She thought it was funny for Podge to want baby clothes, but imagined that Mrs Gray had got someone she was looking after in the village. Podge gave the clothes to Amanda.

Amanda couldn't help feeling important. She thought she had managed her job very well indeed – much better than poor Micky, who had had another talk with Fellin, but with no success at all. 'He's gone home with Midge, threatening him with another thrashing for chasing that silly hen again,' said Micky gloomily. 'That bird seems to strut in front of Midge on purpose. Well, I'll have to keep on at Fellin, I suppose, and try to make friends with Midge. I shall give him a good meal every day.'

'I'll go down to Mrs Potts tomorrow and take her these things,' said Amanda. 'Isn't it nice to think of how clean and sweet her cottage and baby will be now?'

8

Amanda does a Little Work

Yolande went with Amanda to Mrs Potts the next day. They carried some soap flakes and two cloths that Alice, the Rectory daily help, had given them. They also had the baby clothes done up in a parcel. Mrs Potts was not out at work that morning. She seemed to be bustling round a bit, and the baby was actually in its pram out in the garden.

'Look,' Amanda said proudly, in a low voice. 'Mrs Potts has turned over a new leaf already. It shows how easy it is to get things done when you go about them the right way.'

Yolande was impressed. She hadn't thought that the lazy Amanda would really have managed to influence Mrs Potts so soon. But Amanda's ideas were wrong. It was nothing to do with her that Mrs Potts was bustling around, taking down her dirty curtains. Mrs Potts had a smile on her face as she opened the door to the two girls.

'I've had a letter from my husband,' she told them. 'Fancy, he's coming home soon!

He's been halfway round the world!'

'Oh,' said Amanda. 'So that's why you are getting busy, is it? To welcome him home?'

'That's right,' answered Mrs Potts. 'My Ted was proud of this cottage and garden. See that rose-tree there in the middle of the front garden? Well, he planted that for me. A red rose means "I love you", you know.'

Amanda and Yolande didn't know. They thought it was a very nice idea to plant a red rose-tree to show that you loved someone.

'Won't he be pleased to see the baby?' said Amanda. 'Can I take her out this morning, Mrs Potts? And oh, look – we've brought you some soap and two cloths – and there are some lovely clothes for Emily in this parcel.'

Mrs Potts seemed rather touched. 'Thank you,' she said. 'I'll use the soap today, seeing as how I'm going to have a good clean-up. And my, won't Emily look sweet in those things? That's real kind of you.'

'When is Mr Potts coming home?' asked Yolande, most interested in everything.

'Oh, he'll just turn up any time,' said Mrs Potts. 'When his ship gets in, he'll come rolling up. My, it will be grand to see him after all this long time. I'd given him up!'

She dumped the curtains into a tub of hot water, shook in some of Amanda's soap flakes, and began to rub the curtains. But she hadn't rubbed more than half a minute before she put her hand to her side, turned pale, and sat down suddenly.

'What's the matter?' asked Amanda, surprised.

'I've come over peculiar again,' said Mrs Potts. 'Now I shall have to lie down for a bit. And those curtains just in that hot water too. What a waste!'

Leaving the tub in the kitchen, she lay down on a rickety sofa at one side of the sitting-room. The baby outside wailed suddenly.

'Aren't you going to Emily?' said Amanda, who couldn't bear to hear a baby crying.

'It's her teeth again,' said Mrs Potts, not moving. Her eyes were shut. 'She wants a rusk to bite on, I expect. See if there are any in that tin over there, will you?'

'Shall I take her out of the pram and nurse her?' asked Amanda eagerly, longing to hold the baby again.

'No,' Mrs Potts replied. 'You give her a rusk and jog her a bit. Oh, those curtains! I'd made up my mind to do them today – and now I can't.'

Amanda found a rusk and took it out to the baby, who stopped crying and blinked long, tear-wet eyelashes at her.

'Yolande, isn't she lovely?' said Amanda. 'If

79

only she wasn't so pale! You jog her a bit while I go and see if Mrs Potts is any better. Don't let her choke herself on the rusk.'

Feeling rather important, Yolande kept an eye on the baby and jogged the pram: Emily loved it and crowed loudly.

Amanda went back to Mrs Potts, who was still on the sofa, her hand pressed to her side. She opened her eyes when Amanda came in.

'It's a shame to waste that hot soapy water,' sighed Mrs Potts, in rather a weak voice. 'Couldn't you just have a go at them curtains for me? They're thin and don't need much doing.'

Amanda stared at Mrs Potts in dismay. What, wash curtains? She had never washed anything in her life, not even a hair-ribbon or her dolls' clothes. Housework of any sort was not welcomed by Amanda.

Mrs Potts saw her look of dismay. 'What's up?' she said. 'Can't you wash clothes? How old are you? My, when I was your age I could do all the family wash and iron it too. It won't do you any harm to wash out those curtains, will it? I'd do them myself only I feel that ill.'

Mrs Potts did look ill. Amanda looked at the tub of steaming water in the kitchen. The curtains smelled horrid. She wrinkled up her nose in disgust. She couldn't bear even to put her hands in the water!

But, after all, she was a Put-Em-Right, wasn't she? And if she could help by washing dirty curtains, then she ought to do so. So Amanda ran out to Yolande and spoke to her.

'I'm going to wash those curtains for Mrs Potts. You take the baby out for a walk, Yolande, and mind you don't bump her too much.'

Yolande stared in amazement. Amanda going to wash curtains! Goodness gracious, what next? Yolande's look changed to one of admiration. Amanda certainly was being a fine Put-Em-Right!

'Good for you, Mandy,' she said, and wheeled the baby out of the gate, rather proud to be in charge. Amanda went back to the dark, dingy kitchen. She plunged her hands into the water and took hold of the curtains. They were certainly very dirty, but, on the other hand, they were so thin and flimsy that it was easy to get the dirt out of them. Amanda washed busily, hating the smell of soap and dirt.

'You want to rinse them well in the sink when you've finished,' came Mrs Potts's voice from the sitting-room. 'Then wring them as dry as you can, and peg them out on the line.'

Amanda rinsed them till the soap was out. Then she took the wet bundle in her arms and found the pegs. Even the pegs were filthy and Amanda had to wash them before she could use

them. She wasn't going to have the clean curtains made dirty by messy pegs!

She pegged up the curtains and looked at
them with pride. She hadn't liked the work, but
now that it was done she liked seeing the result.

Just then Podge and Micky came by, on their way to the shops. They saw Amanda in the garden and waved. 'How are you getting on? Where's Yo?'

'Yo's taken the baby out,' Amanda said, importantly. 'See these curtains on the line? I've just washed them for Mrs Potts and hung them out. Don't they look nice?'

Micky stared at Amanda in astonishment. He had never known her do a job like that before. 'You see, Mrs Potts isn't feeling well, and the curtains were in the hot soapy water and ready to be done,' said Amanda, enjoying the boys' surprise. 'Mrs Potts will be well enough to do everything herself tomorrow, I expect. Her husband is coming home soon, so she wants everything to be nice.'

Yolande came back with the baby, which now had a little pink in its cheeks from the airing. The boys bent over it. Podge screwed up his nose. 'Bit smelly,' he said, 'and isn't it dirty? Doesn't it ever have a bath? Why don't you wipe its nose, Yo?'

'Wipe it yourself!' said Amanda, from the garden. Podge did. The baby gurgled at him. Podge had never taken any notice of babies before, but he rather liked this one. Micky had seen too many babies brought to the Rectory to be interested. What interested him far more was the sight of Amanda pegging up curtains.

The boys went on their way. Yolande put the pram in the garden and Amanda went in to see Mrs Potts.

She was still on the sofa, but she looked a little better. 'The curtains are on the line,' said Amanda. 'I must go now, Mrs Potts. I'll come along and take the baby out tomorrow, when you're at work. Will you be able to get your cottage nice and tidy for your husband, if you have to go out to work too?'

'I shall do my best,' said Mrs Potts. 'And I must see to that garden, too. I can't have Ted see his rose-tree all choked up with weeds like that, can I?'

'Oh no,' answered Amanda. Then, as a Put-Em-Right, she added a few words. 'The baby will soon look so nice, Mrs Potts, when you get her clean and dressed up, and the cottage will look sweet when you've done a spring-clean. You'll wonder how you put up with its being so dirty once you've got it clean and nice.'

These few words did not please Mrs Potts. 'I don't want no preaching,' she said sourly. 'I'll keep my cottage and my baby how I want to. It's a free country.'

Amanda was puzzled by the remark about the 'free country'. People often seemed to say that when they wanted to go their own way and do things they shouldn't. She said goodbye politely and then she and Yolande went off, very pleased with themselves.

'You know, I really think we've done something there,' said Amanda. 'I believe Mrs Potts will be quite different now!'

9

Podge loses his Bicycle

Sally couldn't help being a little jealous when she heard what good Put-Em-Rights Amanda and Yolande had been. But she sneered a little when Yolande told her how Mrs Potts had asked Amanda to do the curtains.

'Don't get taken in like that!' she said to Amanda. 'She's lazy, is young Mrs Potts! Everyone knows that! She probably just lay down on the sofa and pretended to feel ill so that she could get you to do the washing for her and Yolande to take out the baby.'

'You're not to say things like that,' said Podge at once. 'You'll only make things harder for Amanda. It's un-Christian and just the opposite of what we Put-Em-Rights ought to think. Have a little more kindness, Sally, and not so much hardness.'

Sally felt that she could have slapped Podge. Here she was, trying not to let Amanda be too much taken in and imposed on – and Podge was saying she was hard and unkind!

'You mind your own business,' said Sally, bad-temperedly. 'Wait till you have something to put right, Claude Paget! I'm only trying to help Amanda.'

'She called me Claude so she must be very cross again,' remarked Podge to the others, who couldn't help grinning at his raised eyebrows and mock horror. Sally made an impatient noise and got up.

'It would be better for the Put-Em-Rights if some people weren't members,' she said sharply and walked off. Yolande began to go after her but Podge pulled her down.

'Let her go,' he said. 'She'll probably be all right when her turn comes. She would love to run everything herself, and she can't bear to see Amanda running Mrs Potts like this, and doing it well. That's the worst of these really efficient people. They don't like seeing others doing something successfully!'

'Well, Mrs Potts *did* look ill today,' said Amanda, anxious to prove herself in the right. 'But you'll see, Podge, when I go to see her tomorrow, I guess she'll have the cottage beginning to look really nice!'

'How did you get on with Fellin and Midge today?' said Yolande, remembering the other job on hand.

'Oh, about the same,' Micky said. 'It will be

a long job, I can see – can't expect such quick results as Mandy gets! I fed Midge again today, and got two wags of his tail instead of one. And I told Fellin ever so many times what a fine dog I thought Midge could be.'

'Fellin must think you're cracked about his dog,' said Bobby. 'You'll end in making him think it's a champion or something!'

'No, I shan't,' said Micky, rather gloomily. 'He thinks Midge is awful, and keeps saying so. And nothing I say or do so far will stop him kicking the poor creature or hitting him if he feels like it.'

'I wish something else would turn up now, so that I could have a turn,' said Podge. 'I'm the oldest of you and I'd like to do my share soon.'

'I expect we'll all be busy before many days have gone by,' said Amanda. 'We shall hear of something.'

The children were lying in the big field outside the Rectory garden. It was a favourite place of theirs, for the grass was long and the big oak trees were shady. The church clock struck four – teatime. Yolande was having tea with Amanda and Micky. Podge had to go back home because one of his uncles was coming. He got up to go, and so did the others. Bobby waited to see if Micky would ask him to tea but he didn't. He set off by himself. Podge called to him, saying he was going home too and would walk part of the way with him. He caught up with Bobby and the two went down the lane together.

'I thought you had your bike with you this morning,' said Bobby, suddenly remembering. 'Yes, you did. What have you done with it? Did you leave it in the Rectory shed?'

'Golly, no!' said Podge, stopping. 'I left it against the hedge in the field where we talked. Blow! I forgot all about it. Well, I shan't bother about it now. I'll get it tomorrow.'

Bobby was horrified. What, leave a perfectly good bicycle out in the fields all night? It might be stolen.

'It'll be stolen. You know there's been thefts in the village, don't you? Tools have been taken, and all kinds of things. Your bike may go too.'

'Well, I can't be bothered to go back and get it,' Podge said carelessly. 'If it's stolen, Dad will have to buy me a new one, that's all!'

Bobby thought Podge was wrong and silly to talk like that; but fancy not minding if a bike was stolen! Bobby had never had a bike. He felt jealous and resentful when he thought of Podge having as many as he liked. He was sure Podge had had plenty of bicycles already. He asked him.

'How many bikes have I had? Oh, about four,'

said Podge, as if that was nothing. 'I've had one stolen already. Never got it back either. But don't you worry, Bobby, mine will be all right in that field.'

All the same Bobby did worry about that bike. He was so used to taking the very greatest care of the few things he had that it really hurt him to think of Podge's bike out there in the field. It might pour with rain again. After he had had his tea he made up his mind to go back to the field and get the bike himself. Then he would ride it over to Four Towers and give it back to Podge.

In that way he would make Podge grateful to him, would be able to pay an extra visit to Four Towers, which he loved, and would be able to ride Podge's expensive bike through the village streets so that all the boys might see him. It seemed a very good idea to Bobby. He set out after tea to go back to the Rectory field. He went in at the gate and looked round, trying to remember where Podge had left his bike. Yes, over there, in that hedge, he thought, and went over to it.

But the bicycle wasn't there. Well, he must have made a mistake. He had only got to go carefully round the hedge till he found the bike. Bobby examined the hedge closely as he walked round the field. To his amazement, there was

no bike to be seen. How strange! Could Podge have gone back and got it, then, even though he had said he wouldn't bother? Or perhaps one of the Rectory children had fetched it. He heard Micky's voice in the Rectory garden and called to him. 'Micky! Have you or Amanda fetched Podge's bike from the field?'

'No!' shouted Micky, his face appearing over the garden wall. 'We didn't even know he had left it there. He really is a careless fellow. He'll lose it one day.'

'Well, I came back to get it for him, meaning

to take it over to Four Towers,' said Bobby, 'and it's gone. I wonder if Podge fetched it himself.'

'Shouldn't think so, or he'd have come in for a minute,' said Micky.

'Then it's been stolen,' said Bobby. 'Someone must have pinched it. I'll run across to Four Towers and find out if Podge did come over for it.'

He went over to Podge's home and found the boy in the garden, with a pile of ripe plums beside him, reading a book. Podge was surprised and not too pleased to see Bobby. All the Put-Em-Rights felt that he pushed himself forward too much.

'Hello, Podge,' said Bobby. 'I say, did you fetch your bike from the field?'

'Course not,' said Podge. 'I wasn't going to wear myself out going back for that. I'll get it tomorrow. Why?'

'Well, I went to get it for you, and it's gone,' said Bobby. 'It must have been stolen. Come back and see.'

A little more upset than he showed, Podge went back to the field, and the two boys hunted again. There was no doubt about it, the bike was gone.

'Blow! Now I'll have to tell my dad,' said Podge. 'Lucky my birthday is coming along soon. I'll ask him for a new one.'

'And lose that in about four weeks' time, I suppose,' said Bobby, sneeringly. 'I've never had a bike to lose. Well, yours is gone, Podge. No doubt about that.'

Although Podge was an irresponsible, careless boy, he did not shirk telling his father about the bicycle, nor did he hide the fact that he had left it in the field and come home without it.

His father was annoyed. 'That means a new bicycle, I suppose,' he said, 'and having the police up, and wasting my time.'

So the village policeman came up, big and burly in his dark blue uniform, notebook and pencil in hand. He wrote a detailed account of the bicycle and promised to do what he could to get it back.

'Been a lot of thefts lately,' he said, and shut his notebook. 'Yes, and I have my suspicions, too. I hope, Mr Paget, it won't be long before I put my hand on the thief.'

'I hope you will,' said Mr Paget. 'Got to stop things like that, you know.'

Podge's mother was very sympathetic to him over the loss of his bicycle. She spoilt Podge terribly, and fussed over him quite ridiculously.

'Darling, you can borrow my bicycle,' she said. 'Take it whenever you want it.'

'What do you want to let him do that for?' growled his father. 'Want to encourage him to lose yours, too?'

'Oh, he didn't get his bicycle stolen on purpose, Richard!' said Mrs Paget, looking hurt. 'Don't be so unkind. Boys will be boys, you know.'

'Well, I hope some of them are a bit more careful than Podge, that's all I can say,' said Mr Paget, and then proceeded to say quite a lot more. Podge listened impatiently. He never worried about losing anything: there was always plenty more in the shops!

But as it happened, the bicycle was discovered the very next day. Mr Philpot, the policeman, feeling rather pleased to be working on a case raised by the Pagets of Four Towers, made tremendous efforts, followed up his previous suspicions, and tracked, not only the bicycle, but the other stolen goods as well, to a shed belonging to a family living not far from Four Towers itself.

He brought the bicycle to be seen by Podge, who at once knew it was his. No damage had been done to it. The boy was pleased and jumped on it to ride off to the Rectory to tell the others. He left his father to go into the matter of the theft and did not bother his head any more about it.

'Well, you are a lucky chap!' said Bobby, when he heard. 'Now, if I had a bike and lost it, I know very well I'd never get it back!'

'You be careful of it now, Podge, or you'll keep Mr Philpot busy all the summer,' warned Amanda.

'Well, that little affair is finished,' said Podge. 'So don't let's talk any more about it. The bike was stolen and has been found, and that's all there is to it!'

But there was a lot more than that, as Podge soon found out.

10

A Morning of Happenings

The same day that Podge's bicycle was found Amanda had a shock. She went down to Mrs Potts to take the baby out as she had promised, expecting to see a beautifully clean cottage and a fresh, sweet-smelling baby. But all she found was the same dirty little place, and the same smelly little baby. It was terribly disappointing. She remembered what Sally had said – that Mrs Potts had not meant to turn over a new leaf at all, hadn't been ill, but had just imposed on Amanda and got her to do the washing.

Amanda felt cross. Good gracious, there were the curtains still out on the line too! She went and knocked at the door. Mrs Potts was in her kitchen, in a dirty old dressing-gown. She didn't look well.

'I'm right pleased to see you,' she said to Amanda. 'I've been so ill all night. I reckon I'll have to have the doctor.'

'Oh,' said Amanda, 'I'm so sorry. What's the matter?'

'I don't rightly know,' said Mrs Potts, and she pressed her hand against her side. 'There's a pain here, and I feel so sick. I can hardly drag myself about. And there's my Ted coming home and all, and I did so want to get things nice for him!'

To Amanda's great dismay the young woman sank down on a chair, put her hands over her face and wept loudly. Amanda felt awkward.

'Don't cry so,' she said at last. 'I'll get the doctor to you.'

'They'll take me away to hospital, I know they will!' wept poor Mrs Potts. 'Then what'll happen to my cottage and my baby, and Ted when he comes home?'

'Haven't you anyone you could get in to

help?' said Amanda. 'What about one of the neighbours?'

'They've their hands full and they don't like me,' wept Mrs Potts, talking to Amanda as if she were her own age. 'They think I'm dirty and lazy – but it's not that. I haven't felt well for months, and how can I turn round and do my own home when I'm cleaning other people's all day long and get back tired out?'

'What about your mother? Wouldn't she come and help you?' said Amanda, feeling very sorry for the unhappy young woman.

'My mother's got too many little ones to see to, without bothering with me and my Emily,' said Mrs Potts, drying her eyes. 'But she might send Francie to me, though. That's an idea.'

'Who's Francie?' asked Amanda.

'Francie's one of my young sisters,' said Mrs Potts. 'But older than you, I daresay. She could come and do round a bit and see to Emily. She's had to manage Ma's latest baby for her, so she knows how to do for Emily. But she needs watching, does Francie.'

'Why?' asked Amanda, surprised.

'Oh, she sits about and lazes if she gets the chance,' said Mrs Potts. 'You go over to my mother's for me, there's a duck, and tell her to come along and see me. And ask the doctor to come in, will you?'

Amanda found out where Mrs Potts's mother lived, and set off. She went to Sally's house and borrowed her bicycle, saying mysteriously that she wanted it for Put-Em-Right work. She called in at the doctor's on the way and told him about Mrs Potts. He was an old friend of hers. All the children liked old Dr Harris.

'I'll be by there soon and I'll pop in,' he said. 'She doesn't sound too good to me.'

Then Amanda rode off to the next village where Mrs Tomms, Mrs Potts's mother, lived. She found the little house and looked at the swarm of children in the street outside. Surely all these couldn't belong to Mrs Tomms! But most of them did. Anyway, about six of them went with her to the door of the house when she asked if Mrs Tomms lived there.

Mrs Tomms was an enormously fat woman, with an apron tied tightly round her middle and her hair drawn back into a black and grey bun. She had a glistening red face and a funny little puddingy nose. She eyed Amanda in surprise.

'Are you Mrs Tomms?' asked Amanda. 'I'm Amanda Gray, from the Rectory in the next village. Your daughter, Mrs Potts, is ill, and she says can you spare time to come over and see her, please?'

'Lands sakes and it's my busy day!' said Mrs Tomms. 'Never mind. Hey, Francie, where are

99

you? You come along here and keep an eye on the dinner for me, and look after the children. Come along, now. FRANCIE!'

Francie appeared at last from the back garden, a skinny, sulky-looking girl, bigger than Amanda. She stared at Amanda, and Amanda stared back.

'Did you hear what I said?' demanded Mrs Tomms, taking off her apron and putting a black hat on her head. 'I'll skin you if I come back and find the dinner spoilt.'

Francie scowled. Mrs Tomms set off with Amanda, who now had to wheel her bicycle very slowly as Mrs Tomms poured out to Amanda her family history, and Amanda learned about Ted in the Navy, who was Mrs Potts's husband, and lazy Francie, and mischievous Harry, and the latest Tomms baby, who was called Gideon. She listened with the greatest interest.

'I suppose you thought poor Rene was a proper lazy, dirty piece, keeping her cottage like that and the baby so dirty,' panted Mrs Tomms. 'But Rene was never like that before she married, I can tell you. A good girl she was, and kept herself spick and span. But she's not well. That's it, you know. She's not well.'

Amanda guessed that Rene was Mrs Potts. Mrs Tomms rambled on. 'A better girl than Rene you couldn't see, and a right smart boy

Ted is too. Poor girl, she got so down never hearing from him. She let herself go to pieces, and the house too, instead of seeing the doctor and getting things put right. Obstinate, that's what she is. Always afraid of having to go to hospital, though I must say when I was there I properly enjoyed myself. Only time in my life I've ever been fussed round.'

'Ted's coming back soon,' said Amanda, pleased at having a bit of news for Mrs Tomms.

'There now!' said Mrs Tomms. 'What did I tell Rene? Didn't I say, "My girl, one of these here days your Ted will turn up all unexpected-like, and what he'll think of you and your dirty house and baby I don't know! You pull yourself together," I told her. But she never would listen to me.'

'I do hope Rene will be able to get everything nice for Ted when he does come home,' said Amanda. 'It would be awful for him to come back and find everything in such a mess. And his rose-tree all choked with weeds.'

'That was real nice of him, wasn't it, to plant that red rose there,' said Mrs Tomms, stopping for breath. 'Ah, he's a nice boy, Ted is.'

They talked on and on. Mrs Tomms didn't talk to Amanda as if she was a child. She made Amanda feel very grown-up and important, especially when she praised her for being a good

friend to Rene. When they arrived in sight of
Mrs Potts's cottage they got a shock. A big
ambulance stood outside!

'Oh, gracious, they're not taking my Rene
away, are they!' cried Mrs Tomms, and actually
burst into a run. The doctor was at the gate and
a nurse was just going into the little cottage with
him.

'Ah, Mrs Tomms,' he said, 'I'm afraid your

daughter is very ill. She must go to hospital at once. The baby could perhaps go home to you for a few weeks?'

'Oh, my poor daughter! Oh, she'll get better all right, won't she?' panted Mrs Tomms, tears suddenly running down her cheeks.

'Of course, of course,' said Dr Harris, and patted her gently on the shoulder. 'Now, you go in and have a word with her before she goes.'

'You come too,' said Mrs Tomms to Amanda. So the two went in together, Amanda suddenly feeling rather frightened and upset.

'Oh, Ma!' cried Mrs Potts, as her mother came in at the door. 'Oh, Ma! What am I to do? Will you have Emily for me? Can you send Francie to clean up here, because Ted's coming back and he must have somewhere to go? Oh, Ma, *what* am I to do?'

Mrs Potts seemed to have changed from a young woman into a tearful child. She clung to her mother, who patted her.

'Now, now, don't you take on so, you'll soon be back and as right as rain. I knew there was something wrong with you. It wasn't like you to let things go like you did. But don't you worry, I'll have Emily, and I'll send Francie over every day to get this place cleaned up and nice for Ted.'

'Ma, Francie won't do it by herself,' moaned

Rene. 'Can't you keep an eye on her?'

'Now you know I can't, with all the little ones to see to at home,' said Mrs Tomms. 'But I'll tell Francie I'll skin her good and proper if she doesn't do things right.'

Mrs Potts suddenly turned to Amanda. 'You come along and see that Francie does things right,' she begged. 'I trust you, see? You keep an eye on Francie for me. You promise me that.'

Amanda could do nothing else but promise, though the idea of keeping an eye on the older, sulky-looking Francie was not at all tempting. But she felt so desperately sorry for the ill woman that she felt glad to give her any peace of mind.

'Let Francie bring Emily over with her each morning,' said Amanda. 'I love Emily. The airing will be good for her too.'

'I'll do that,' promised Mrs Tomms. 'Now just don't you worry about anything, Rene, my girl. You'll be all right, and back at home again in a couple of jiffs. And everything will be ready for Ted. Now – here's the doctor and nurse. You let them help you, and be a good girl and do everything they say.'

Poor Rene was lifted into the ambulance, crying loudly. Emily, in her pram, lifted up her voice and wailed too. The driver set his engine going, and the ambulance jolted slowly away down the lane, disappearing round a corner.

'Well!' said Mrs Tomms, sitting down very suddenly. 'This is a bit of an upset. I could do with a cup of tea.'

Her poor fat face crumpled up and, to Amanda's dismay, she saw that Mrs Tomms was crying like a child. 'I'll make you a cup of tea,' she said with a rush of warm kindness. Amanda had never boiled a kettle in her life, but she put one on the stove and lit the gas.

'You're a kind child,' said Mrs Tomms, wiping her tears with a red-spotted handkerchief. 'Yes, and your mother's kind, too. Many's the tale I've heard of her and your father, the good Rector.'

Amanda glowed. It was nice to hear things like that about her parents. She looked round for a teapot.

'Here, you want to warm it first,' said Mrs Tomms. 'Put a drop of hot water in. That's right. There's the tea-caddy, look. Lor' bless the child, if she isn't going to put the tea in without pouring away the water first!'

Mrs Tomms emptied the teapot, put in three big teaspoonfuls of tea, and then poured the boiling water into the teapot. She stirred the tea round with a spoon and put the lid on.

Amanda got cups and saucers and found some milk. She thought it would be very nice and grown-up to sit and have a cup of tea with Mrs

Tomms. But she wished she hadn't when Mrs
Tomms poured out the tea; it was terribly
strong. Amanda could hardly swallow it.

'Ah, this makes me feel better,' said Mrs
Tomms. 'A lot better. Nothing like a cup of tea,
good and strong. Well, I'll take little Emily back
with me now, and I'll send my Francie over in
the morning. She can come over every day till
this dirty place is cleaned up. My, it wants some
doing too! And that garden! It's a fair sight, it's
so choked with weeds!'

'It really is dreadful, isn't it?' said Amanda.
'And it could be so pretty too.'

'Well, now, will you really come along and

keep an eye on my Francie?' asked Mrs Tomms. 'She just won't work if she's alone. Goes mooning round or reads a book. But if you pop in sometimes, she'll keep at it. My Rene seemed to think a lot of you, didn't she?'

Amanda flushed. She didn't particularly want to 'keep an eye on Francie'. She felt that Francie would object very strongly. But she had promised, and it was unthinkable not to keep her word. So she nodded.

'Yes. I'll come down each day and see how Francie is getting on.'

'And you tell me if she's lazy,' said Mrs Tomms, not guessing that she was talking to another lazy little girl.

'I should think Francie would feel pleased at getting everything nice for Ted, and for Rene to come back to,' said Amanda, taking another gulp of the strong tea, and wishing she could spit it out. 'No, thank you, Mrs Tomms, I won't have another cup.'

'I'll send Emily over with her each day,' said Mrs Tomms. She caught sight of some baby clothes hanging on an airer. 'My! Where did those come from? Aren't they lovely? Emily would look fine in those!'

'A friend of mine gave them to me for Emily,' explained Amanda. 'I thought she would look sweet in them, too.'

They talked about Emily for a little while and Mrs Tomms had her third cup of tea. Then she rose. 'Well, I must get back and see to dinner. Thank you, for all your kindness and help. You're like your mother, you are!'

She went off, wheeling Emily in her pram. Amanda sped back to the Rectory, excited. What a tale she had to tell the others! What a lot of things had happened to her that morning, and how good it was to help to put them right! The others would be quite envious of her!

11

Podge's Turn Now

When Amanda got back to the Rectory she found that it was lunch-time, that her mother and father were out, and that the whole of the Put-Em-Rights were impatiently waiting for her to return because they were going to have a picnic in the garden.

'Gosh! We thought you were never coming!' said Micky. 'What have you been doing?'

'What do you think? We've got another case to put right!' said Yolande, her eyes dancing. 'It's something for the boys this time, so either Podge or Bobby have got to do it.'

Yolande was thrilled because once again her turn had not come. Amanda longed to tell her story and was just beginning it when Podge hustled them all into the garden.

'We'll hear everything there,' he said. 'Go on, help to carry these things, Amanda! I know you're bursting with news. So are we!'

When they were sitting down, eating ham sandwiches and juicy red tomatoes from the greenhouse, there was a lot of excited talk.

'Let's tell Amanda about our newest case,' said Sally. 'Once she gets going on her adventure, we'll never get a word in! I'm sure she's longing to tell us how Mrs Potts has turned over a new leaf, got her cottage clean, and made the baby look like a princess!'

'Amanda, do you know the Tupps?' asked Podge.

'Yes, they live in Cherry Cottage, the other side of the village, don't they?' said Amanda, remembering. 'I've seen Mrs Tupp in church sometimes – a quiet little woman, with two or three children. One of them's a big boy, rather funny looking.'

'Yes, that's right,' said Podge. 'Well, what do you think? They're being turned out of their cottage at the end of this week and they've nowhere to go, and Mr Tupp's lost his job! They've got no money at all. Isn't it awful?'

'But – can people be turned out like that?' asked Amanda, in horror, thinking what she would feel like if her mother and father, and herself and Micky, and all their belongings were turned out into the road.

'Yes, I suppose so,' replied Podge. 'Anyway, it's perfectly true. Bobby heard all about it from his mother this morning.'

'Oh, dear! But however can we put a big thing

like that right?' said Amanda. 'I mean how can we stop it? Whatever can we do?'

They had all stopped eating as they talked. Sally spoke firmly. 'I think we ought to go to the landlord, whoever he is, and beg him to give them another chance. And we'd better go to the Tupps and find out if they owe rent or something, and try to help them pay it. I've got some money in the post office. I'm sure Mummy would let me take it out for that.'

Micky's heart sank. It seemed as if it was going to be expensive, belonging to the Put-Em-Rights. He didn't want to pay anybody's rent with his money!

'Whose job will this be?' asked Amanda.

'Either Podge's or Bobby's,' said Sally. 'The boys think that if landlords have to be tackled, it is better for them to do it, not us girls. Not that I should mind doing it at all.' Privately she thought that she could do it a good deal better than the boys.

'We'll toss for it,' said Podge to Bobby and he took a coin out of his pocket. 'Heads it's my job this time, and tails it's yours, Bobby.' He threw the coin into the air. It came down with the head uppermost. 'My job,' said Podge.

'I'm glad it's not mine,' said Yolande. 'I should die if I had to go and face a landlord, I know I should. And I'm afraid of Mr Tupp. He's so big and frowny. I could never, never do a thing like this. In fact, I don't believe I'll ever be able to put anything really right. I shall be too scared.'

'You're a baby,' said Podge. 'Well, now let's hear Amanda's tale.'

Amanda began. She told all about the morning's happenings. And the others listened with wide eyes, astonished that so much could have happened to Amanda. They heartily approved of all that the little girl had done.

'You're a very good Put-Em-Right,' said Micky, patting her on the back. 'Now you just keep an eye on Francie and make her get things shipshape in that cottage, and you'll have done your job well – made Mrs Potts happy, got ready a good welcome for Ted, and given them both a good start when they are together again.'

'How did you get on today, Mick?' asked Amanda, her face red with pleasure at the praise given her.

'A bit better,' said Micky. 'I fed Midge again and he licked my hand! You should have seen Fellin's face! He said, "Cor – I never see Midge give a lick before!" I said, "Well, if you show him a bit of kindness he'll give you a lick too." But he didn't show him any kindness that I could see. In fact, he gave him a kick or two when he growled at a hen.'

They finished their picnic and lay down lazily on their backs. Podge wondered if he ought to go and tackle the Tupps. They only had till Saturday to stay in their house, and today was Thursday. There wasn't much time.

'You all think it would be best to go and find out if they're behind with the rent first, and offer to lend them the money, and then go and tell the landlord?' asked Podge, looking round. Everyone nodded.

'Right,' said Podge and got up. He set off down the lane. Bobby yelled after him.

'Podge! Hi, Podge! Aren't you going on your bike, idiot?'

'Gosh, I forgot all about it again,' said Podge, and went to get it.

'You really are careless!' said Sally. 'You deserve to have your things stolen.'

'Yes, teacher!' said Podge, grinning as he mounted his bicycle. He cycled to the Tupps' house. It stood a little way back from the road, not far from Four Towers itself. Podge went up to the door, wondering how to begin.

He knocked. A voice shouted, 'Come in!' Podge opened the door and walked into a hot little kitchen. A big, red-faced man was sitting in a chair, looking gloomily at a table. Not far off was a big lout of a boy, with a miserable face and untidy red hair. He looked about fifteen, and rather odd. The man looked up. He was surprised to see Podge, whom he didn't know at all. 'What do you want?' he asked.

'Er – I just wondered – er – I thought I'd like to ask if you had found anywhere to go on Saturday,' said Podge, his face burning red with embarrassment. He felt that somehow he was going about things the wrong way.

Mr Tupp stared at him. 'What's it to do with you?' he said roughly.

'Well – I was very sorry to hear about it,' replied Podge. 'And I thought – if it was rent or anything – well, er – there are people who might like to help, you know.'

The big boy behind his father's chair made Podge feel awkward. He never took his eyes off Podge, and they were curious, staring eyes. Podge wished he would go out of the room. Mr Tupp seemed puzzled by Podge. He was not used to visitors who came in and talked like this. He scratched his chin with a rasping noise and considered Podge carefully. What made this boy come?

'What's your name?' asked Mr Tupp in a more kindly tone.

'Claude Paget,' said Podge. 'I live at . . .' But he didn't finish his sentence. Mr Tupp stood up suddenly and his face was as black as thunder.

'Are you the son of the man who owns Four

Towers? What, are you? Well – you get out of my house! Go on, get out, before I kick you out! I'm not having any truck with you! What do you come here for? To laugh at me? If I see you here again I'll knock you into the middle of next week! Get out!'

Podge stepped backwards to the doorway. It was all so unexpected. Whatever had made the man behave like this? Podge was completely taken aback. The big boy in the room began to laugh in delight. It was a silly laugh and Podge didn't like it. Mr Tupp went on glaring at him, his face like a beetroot.

'Do you hear what I say?' he shouted, taking a step towards Podge. 'Get out of my house, or I'll put you out!'

'Hee-hee-hee!' laughed the boy behind. Podge saw that there was absolutely nothing to be done but to get out of the house quickly. The man was plainly in a furious temper, though why, Podge could not imagine. After all, he had only come to offer a bit of help.

Podge retreated, glad to be out of the hot little kitchen. The man slammed the door viciously. As he went down the garden path Podge could hear the boy indoors still laughing in his high, silly voice.

Podge felt upset. It was all so unexpected. He couldn't understand it. He walked off down the lane, thinking hard, and then suddenly remembered that he had left his bicycle leaning against the wall outside the Tupps' house. Blow! He always seemed to be forgetting it now. He turned and went back.

When he got there he found the boy staring

in delight at the bike. He was ringing the bell
and he stroked the bright handles.

'Just come back for it,' said Podge, and was
about to take it away from the wall when the
big boy made a snatch at it.

'Stop it,' said Podge, and took the bicycle
away from the lad's reach. He mounted it and
rode off, leaving the boy staring after him.
Podge didn't like having to go back to the others
and admit having such a complete failure
straight off. Micky and Amanda had managed
to get something done. But it looked as if he

not only hadn't put anything right at all, but wasn't going to be able to, either. However could he do anything when Mr Tupp roared at him and turned him out of his house?

Podge found the others. They were still lying on the grass, eating ripe plums which Micky had picked from a tree in the Rectory orchard. Podge rang his bell as he rode up the path and the others sat up in amazement.

'Why, here's Podge back again!' they cried. 'What's happened, Podge?'

'Have you put things right already?' asked Bobby, surprised.

Podge jumped off his bike and threw it down on the ground. He looked gloomy.

'No,' he said. 'I have to report an utter failure; but it wasn't my fault.' He told them what happened.

'Bad luck,' Sally said. 'But we can't leave it like this. Something has got to be done!'

12

Podge
gets a Shock

The children discussed thoroughly all that had happened to Podge: it seemed very strange.

'Well, it doesn't seem the least use trying to get anything out of Mr Tupp, or to help him,' said Micky at last. 'You'd better try the landlord, Podge. If the man is behind with his rent, we could pay the landlord, I suppose.'

Micky ended his little speech with a sigh. He had had to take money out of his money-box for soap flakes for Mrs Potts. He felt he would have to buy Midge a collar, even if only to touch Fellin's hard heart. And now he would have to hand out more for Mr Tupp's rent. Really, it was very hard to be a good Put-Em-Right.

'Yes, Podge could try the Tupps' landlord,' Amanda agreed.

'Who is he? Does anyone know?' asked Podge. 'He won't be quite so fierce to tackle as Tupp, anyway! Mr Tupp honestly seems to have got a bee in his bonnet about something!'

No one knew who the Tupps' landlord was.

'How are we to find out?' wondered Yolande. 'We can't possibly ask Mr Tupp.'

'We might ask Mrs Tupp, or one of the children,' suggested Sally.

'I shan't ask that awful boy,' said Podge. 'I loathe him. You should have heard him laugh – tee-hee-hee – all high and silly, like that. Sally, I wonder if your mother knows anything about him. Maybe he went to her school.'

'No, the Tupps have only been here a year, I think,' said Sally. 'And the boy had left school before they came. He works with his father on the land. The other two, the younger ones, go to school here though.'

'It seems to me that Podge had better ask one of the children who the landlord is,' said Micky. 'You can't give up, Podge. You've got to go on somehow. There's an awful wrong to be put right there.'

'I know,' said Podge. 'I'm not giving up, don't worry. I wish I hadn't tackled Mr Tupp first, though. I feel I've put him against me, somehow, I don't know why. I wish I'd found out who the landlord was, and gone to him first.'

'Well, find out that now,' said Sally. 'You had better get to work on that at once, Podge, hadn't you? You haven't much time before Saturday.'

Podge got up. 'I'll go now,' he said. 'I'll hang

about and see if I can see the Tupp children. If I don't come back, you'll know Pa Tupp has caught me and put me down his well or something!'

Yolande stared after Podge in alarm and began to scramble up. She adored her big cousin and could not bear the idea of him coming to any harm. 'Podge, Podge! Shall I come with you?' she shouted. But Podge was too far away on his bicycle to hear her. Micky pulled her down on to the grass again.

'It's all right, Yo,' he said. 'Podge is only joking. He won't come to any harm. He can look after himself all right.'

Podge rode down to the Tupps' lane again but he didn't go as far as the house this time. He wished he had asked Sally what the Tupp children were like. If they were anything like that awful boy, he would know them all right!

A little girl came down the lane with a puppy. It ran up and licked Podge's legs. 'What a dear little pup!' said Podge to the small girl. 'What's his name?'

'Scamp,' the girl said shyly.

'And what's your name?' asked Podge, hoping it might be Tupp.

'Mary Thomas,' said the girl. Podge was disappointed. She wasn't a Tupp then.

'Do the Tupp children live down here?' he

said, though he knew they did. 'What are they like?'

'They've got red hair, same as their ma,' said the little girl. 'Look! There's Mrs Tupp coming now.'

Podge turned and saw a quiet, worried-looking woman coming along the lane, carrying a very heavy basket. She had red hair and a lot of freckles, and was very like the big boy Podge had seen with Mr Tupp. As she came near Podge, she set the basket down with a sigh and leaned against a gate to have a rest.

'Shall I carry the basket for you?' asked Podge. 'I could balance it on the seat of my bike.'

'Oh, no, thank you,' said Mrs Tupp. 'I've only got a little way to go now.'

'Oh, do you live down this lane, then?' said Podge, trying to find some way to get into close conversation with Mrs Tupp so that he could ask her about her landlord.

'Yes, in the last cottage,' said Mrs Tupp. 'But we shan't be there much longer. We're being turned out. It's very hard because we don't know where to go.'

'It's a shame!' said Podge. 'It really is. I'm most terribly sorry about it. I wish I could help.'

Mrs Tupp glanced at the boy in surprise. 'Well, nobody can,' she said. 'I've just been to the landlord to beg him to give us another chance. But he won't. A right hard man he is!'

'He must be a beast,' said Podge.

'All he's done is to give me another week to find somewhere to go; and then, if I can't, he says he'll send men to turn all my furniture into the road,' said Mrs Tupp. 'Another week! How am I to find somewhere in a week? And I can tell you, people aren't anxious to have a family that's been turned out!'

'Your landlord ought to be sent to prison!' declared Podge, stoutly. 'Who is this awful man? I'll tell my father about him!'

Then Podge got the shock of his life.

'Our landlord is Mr Paget of Four Towers,' said Mrs Tupp. 'It's him who's turning us out. He's a hard man and there's no moving him. I had to beg almost on my bended knees for another week.'

Podge went pale. His own father! He hadn't expected that. He stared at Mrs Tupp, unable to say a single word. She picked up her basket again. Podge walked beside her down the lane, swallowing hard, trying to think of something to say. Should he tell her who he was? Should he say he would go to his father and beg him to let the Tupps off, so that they might stay? But would his father listen to him?

He didn't see Mr Tupp coming up the lane to meet Mrs Tupp. But Mr Tupp saw him. He made a noise like an angry tiger, and then let out a yell that made both Podge and Mrs Tupp jump.

'What's the matter, John?' asked Mrs Tupp in alarm. Mr Tupp pointed a finger at Podge.

'See him? He's Paget's boy! His father's the one who's turning us out! I've sent him off once, and now he's here again. I'll shake him till his teeth rattle.'

In the greatest alarm Podge got on his bicycle and rode off. His head was in a whirl. No wonder Mr Tupp had flown into such a temper when he had heard Podge's name! Oh, gosh! So it was his own father who was the landlord! What a muddle! He wouldn't dare to go near the Tupps again, that was certain. Poor Podge! He didn't

at all like going back to tell the others what had happened this time. They had all been so certain that the landlord must be a perfect brute – and Podge knew his father was anything but that. Yet what could make him so hard-hearted as to threaten to throw out the Tupps so soon?

Podge went for a long and lonely bicycle ride, trying to reason things out. Did his father know how horrid he must seem to outsiders? Did he know what a terrible thing it must seem to the Tupps to be turned out like that? Ought Podge to tell him? When at last Podge went back to the Rectory, only Micky and Amanda were there. He was glad. He didn't really want to discuss his father's doings with either Sally or Bobby, and he knew Yolande would be very upset. They would all have to know sooner or later, for it had been agreed that the Put-Em-Rights should discuss everything with one another. But Podge didn't want to just then.

'What's up, Podge?' asked Micky when the boy strolled into the room where Micky and Amanda were reading. It had begun to rain so the others had gone home, and Micky and Amanda were indoors.

'Have you found out who the landlord is?' demanded Amanda.

'Yes,' said Podge. 'It's my father.'

There was a startled silence. Micky and Amanda stared wide-eyed at Podge.

'Gosh!' Micky exclaimed. 'That rather messes things up, doesn't it?'

Podge told them how he had found out.

'The Tupps have got another week's grace,' he said. 'I suppose I'd better tackle Dad, hadn't I? Offer to pay the back rent, or something? But it doesn't seem very like Dad to do a thing like this just because someone is behind with their rent. I can't understand it. We've got plenty of money and Dad is always so generous.'

'Yes, you'll have to talk to your father, I suppose,' said Micky. 'But isn't it awfully awkward? I mean – fathers and mothers don't like their children interfering in their affairs. Will your father go up in smoke?'

'I expect so,' said Podge gloomily. 'He's going away for the weekend, so I'll have to wait till Monday when he's back. I don't like this hanging over me all the weekend!'

'No, it's awful,' said Amanda sympathetically. 'But I don't see that you can do anything about it till your father comes back. I'm sorry for you, Podge.'

All the Put-Em-Rights were sorry for Podge when they heard. They could see the whole thing had been a shock for him. They dropped the subject for a few days, agreeing not to mention it to Podge.

Little Yolande was more worried than anyone. She loved her Uncle Dick, and couldn't imagine how such a nice kind uncle could turn people out into the road. She worried about Podge, too, in case he got into a row with his father. Uncle Dick was easy-going as a rule – but if he lost his temper he shouted and banged, and Yolande was afraid of that.

Micky tried to interest the others in Midge the next day. The boy was really getting quite fond of the little dog. 'You know, he's really only a pup still,' he said. 'Not quite six months old. He's got plenty of play and nonsense in him if only he wasn't so frightened. Fellin lets me take him off with me now when I go for a walk, and Midge follows like anything! And I'm going to buy Midge a collar. I think he'll look nice in a brown leather collar with brass studs on it.'

It looked as if Micky's money-box would soon be very much lighter!

13

Amanda
and Francie

Amanda set off the next day to Mrs Potts's cottage to 'keep an eye on Francie'. She didn't want to do this at all, but the others all insisted that she must carry out her promise. Indeed, Amanda herself knew she must. Lazy and selfish as she often was, she never broke her word.

She couldn't imagine how she was going to keep Francie up to the mark, if the older girl slacked or shirked. The cottage really must be cleaned properly, everything washed, and the garden done. She couldn't possibly order Francie about. And how would Francie take it if she, Amanda, sat down and watched all the time to make sure she was getting on?

'I know. I could take Emily out in the pram, and tell Francie that it would be lovely to see things looking better when I come back,' said Amanda to herself. 'That's what I'll do.'

She came to Mrs Potts's cottage and saw that Emily was in the front garden in her pram. The pram was quite still so Amanda thought the baby must be asleep, and she tiptoed over to look at her. She was fast asleep, one small hand above her head, the other clutching a half-eaten rusk.

'She's asleep!' called Francie's voice. 'Don't you wake her now. She'll yell her head off if you do, and I can tell you she gave us an awful night last night. Yelled all the time. I'm proper sleepy, I am, because I had to have Emily in my room. I'm just having a lie-down on the sofa.'

Amanda took a quick look round. It seemed as if Francie hadn't done a single thing, nor did it look as if she meant to. Mrs Potts was right – Francie was a lazy girl and wouldn't do anything unless she was made to.

'Aren't you going to start work?' said Amanda. 'You'll do one room at a time, won't you? What about this dirty kitchen? The sink is filthy and the floor wants a good scrub.'

'Are you busy this morning?' asked Francie, after a pause, during which she eyed Amanda up and down.

'No,' said Amanda. 'That's why I came down to see if I could take Emily out.'

'Well, I don't want you to,' said Francie. 'Let her sleep. You help me instead.'

Amanda felt alarmed. What, help Francie clean this dirty cottage? She didn't want to in the least: she hated work of any kind. She said nothing.

'Come on. You help, too,' urged Francie. 'I don't like doing things by myself, but I'll work if anyone else does, see? We'll soon get things done if we do them together. It's fun then. But it isn't if you have to slog along by yourself.'

'Well,' said Amanda. 'Well, I'm no good really at housework. I'll just take Emily out – you set to and get on. It's your sister's cottage, after all.'

'Afraid of a bit of hard work, that's what you are,' said Francie rudely.

There was so much truth in this that Amanda was angry.

'I'm not! I could clean up this sitting-room long before you could half-clean that kitchen.'

'You couldn't,' said Francie, in a tone of such utter disbelief that Amanda was angrier than ever. She went red and pursed up her lips.

'All right. We'll see,' she said. 'You're the one that's afraid of hard work, not me. You'd have been on that couch all the morning if I hadn't come along. Come on – I'll just show you I can do better work than you!'

She rolled up her sleeves. Francie stared in surprise. She got off the sofa. 'Here, you'd better wear an overall or something,' she said. 'Your ma won't half be angry if you dirty that clean dress.'

'It's only an old one I wear in the holidays,' said Amanda, still angry, as she looked down at her blue cotton dress with its pretty white spots. Francie took down an old overall of Mrs Potts's from behind the door, and tied it round the furious Amanda.

'I can do it myself, thank you,' said Amanda. 'It might tire you too much to tie the strings!'

'Nasty temper you've got,' remarked Francie amiably. 'There – you look a bit odd, but it don't matter how dirty you get in that!'

Amanda flounced herself away from Francie, still in a rage. She went to the kitchen and looked for a broom to get the cobwebs down from the ceiling. She knew that was the first thing Alice, the daily help at the Rectory, always did when she turned out a room. Francie followed her into the kitchen, turning up her own sleeves.

Amanda went back into the dirty sitting-room with an old broom. She looked at the bits of furniture.

I think I'll take out what furniture I can into the garden, and all the mats too, she thought. Then I'll clean up the sitting-room properly, and put the things back afterwards when I've shaken the mats and polished the furniture.

She staggered out with chairs and a table. She heard Francie running water into a pail. Stupid, lazy girl! Amanda meant to show her up. She would clean the sitting-room long before Francie had done the kitchen!

Amanda got down the many cobwebs from
the ceiling and looked at the grey, webby stuff
in distaste. She shook it out into the garden.
Then she tied a duster over the broom, and
rubbed it vigorously up and down the walls to
clean these. By this time the duster was absolutely black.

'Is there another duster anywhere?' she inquired stiffly of Francie, putting her head into the kitchen where Francie was busy scrubbing the floor.

'No. You'll have to wash that one out if you want another,' said Francie, pushing her hair back from her face. 'There's plenty of hot water in the tap.'

I'll bring some cloths from home, thought Amanda, making up her mind to come back that afternoon. 'I'll never finish this sitting-room if I have to keep on washing out dirty dusters. I'll do them all together at the end.'

She washed the bit of paint there was, and washed the window ledges too. She cleaned the little window inside and out. She tried doing it with soap and water, and got the panes all smeary. Francie laughed at her.

'You don't want to use soap for windows, silly! Use plain water and this old leather, see? That's right!'

It was hard work. Amanda's face got very red and hot. Emily slept peacefully in the garden. Francie could be heard working hard too. She knew how to work when she wanted to. She had had to do plenty for her mother. After about an hour and a half she popped her head in at the sitting-room door.

'Do you want a cup of tea?' she said. 'I

134

could do with one. I'll put the kettle on.'

Amanda was still feeling cross, though not quite so much as she had felt at first. She looked at Francie, whose face was streaked with dirt, and wondered if her own was the same.

'Well, I don't mind; but do you make the tea as strong as your mother does?' asked Amanda. 'It was quite black and tasted horrid.'

'I like my tea strong, too,' said Francie. 'But you can have yours with plenty of milk in if you like. I brought some over with me.'

Francie made some tea. She provided cups but no saucers. The two girls sipped the tea, sitting outside in the sun. It was pleasant to have a little rest.

'Sitting-room's beginning to look like itself,' said Francie.

'Yes,' said Amanda stiffly. 'I can work hard, as you see.'

Francie said nothing. She sipped her tea and poured herself out another cup. It was terribly strong. Then Emily woke up and pulled herself into a sitting position in her pram. She beamed at the two girls. Amanda's heart warmed to her.

'She's a lovely baby,' she said, forgetting to be cross any more.

Francie had had too much to do with babies of all ages and sizes to be very thrilled about Emily.

135

'Mmm,' she said, drinking her tea. 'Do you want to push her out now? You've done a good lot of work in that dirty sitting-room. I can finish it for you.'

'No, thank you,' said Amanda, with much dignity. 'I said I would do the sitting-room and I'm going to.'

'You can't do it all in one day,' said Francie. 'Not if you're going to do it properly.'

Amanda had come to that conclusion herself. The sitting-room was small, but it was extremely dirty and had a lot of things in it, all of which needed to be washed, cleaned or polished.

'I shall come back this afternoon,' she said. 'And I shall come tomorrow, too. In fact, I shall go on coming till the sitting-room is fit for Ted to come back to.'

'Well, it'll be nice to have company,' said Francie, finishing her tea. 'But I guess you won't stick it after this morning. Anyone can see you're not used to work like this. You'll be tired out and fed up – and that's the last I'll see of you.'

'I don't know why you have such a bad opinion of me,' said Amanda, half angry and half hurt. 'I dare say I don't know how to do things in a house as well as you do, but I can do them if I know.'

'Don't go and get high-and-mighty again,' said Francie, grinning at Amanda. 'I like you.'

136

Amanda suddenly felt pleased. She didn't know why she should be glad that this rather sulky, lazy girl should like her, but she was. She began to like Francie, too.

'Do you help your mother, like I have to help mine?' asked Francie. 'You've only got a daily help, haven't you, in that big Rectory? I reckon there's a lot to do.'

Amanda said nothing, because she didn't help her mother at all: she didn't even make her own bed. Her mother had said she must, but all that Amanda did was to drag the sheets and blankets up each day, so Alice now did it for her. She didn't like to admit to Francie that she didn't help her mother at all.

Emily crowed and that changed the subject. 'She's good-tempered after her sleep,' said Francie. 'She looks a bit cleaner, doesn't she? Ma lent her some of our own baby's things. I washed all Emily's clothes before I came this morning. I brought them over here to iron, but we haven't had time yet.'

'I'll help you this afternoon,' said Amanda, thinking it would be fun to iron small baby clothes. 'And I'll bring more dusters and cloths. It's awful having so few. And I couldn't find any polish for the furniture. I'll bring some of that, too.'

Amanda was terribly hungry by the time it

was one o'clock. She sped home to the Rectory, and Francie wheeled Emily back to the next village. Both of them were dirty, tired and hot.

'What *have* you been doing with yourself, Amanda!' cried Mrs Gray when she saw her coming in.

'Just doing a few jobs, Mummy!' called Amanda, disappearing into the bathroom.

Amanda ate an enormous lunch. Even Micky was surprised. She told him what she had been doing. He was even more surprised.

'Well! I'd never have thought you could!' he said. 'The others are coming up this afternoon.

138

They'll have a surprise, too, when you tell them.'

'I can't stay with you and the others long,' said Amanda. 'I've got to get back and finish that sitting-room. I can't have Francie saying I'm shirking.'

'I thought it was you who had to keep an eye on Francie, and not Francie on you!' said Micky.

'Well, I suppose it's nicer for Francie if I keep her company and work with her,' Amanda said seriously. 'And you know, Mick — it's really rather fun to see things getting clean and nice! I rather think I'll tackle the garden, too, later on. If I could get those weeds out it would look so much better. And there are stacks of flowering marigolds there, all hidden by weeds. The garden would really look pretty if I weeded it.'

'I might come along and help you when you begin to do the garden,' said Micky. 'I could bring Midge with me. He likes going out with me now. Don't you think he's getting to be a lovely little dog, Mandy? He looks so much fatter, and his coat's getting quite silky. He doesn't keep his tail down so much, either.'

'I think he looks ever so much nicer,' said Amanda. 'Are you going to get him a collar, Mick? He will look awfully grand with one on. I wish I could help you to buy one, but I'm getting some polish this afternoon, and I expect it will take most of my money. I'm not going to ask the others to help with that, because they helped with the soap flakes.'

'It's expensive, putting things right, isn't it?' said Micky, gloomily.

'Yes, but it's worth it,' said Amanda. 'Here come the others.'

They were very interested when they heard about Amanda and the work she had done. 'Who would think it of our lazy little Amanda!' said Podge. 'How did you manage to keep your dress so clean, Mandy? You don't look as if you've been working hard in a dirty room!'

'Oh, I wore an old overall,' said Amanda. 'And that reminds me – I'll take one of my own and keep it down there. I kept tripping up over Mrs Potts's overall, it was too long.'

'She's plainly going to live down there for the rest of the hols,' said Micky. 'Well, well – being a Put-Em-Right is a full-time job for Amanda, it seems. I hope Ted will be properly grateful when he comes home.'

'I'm going off now,' said Amanda. 'I'll just take an overall, and these cloths, and buy some polish on the way. Goodbye. See you at teatime, everybody!' And off went Amanda, quite looking forward to her afternoon's work!

14

More about
the Tupps

Micky bought Midge a beautiful collar that day.
He spent more money on it than he meant to,
but Midge looked so much nicer in the expensive, dark-green collar than in the cheaper brown
one that Micky felt he really must buy it.

And now I must save harder than ever, and
try to replace all the money I've spent, thought
Micky. He took Midge to show Fellin. Fellin
stared in surprise at the collar.

'Well, now, look at that!' he said. 'That must
have cost you a mint of money, Micky. You must
be downright fond of Midge.'

'I am,' said Micky. 'And anyway, Midge is
almost six months old, isn't he, and ought to
have a collar.' Micky fondled Midge's ears.
Midge rolled over on his back, put all his legs
into the air, and looked so absurd that Micky
laughed. 'You are really getting a playful little
pup!' he said, and tickled Midge underneath.

Fellin came back with the barrow. He looked
in surprise at the playful dog. 'Never seen Midge

do that before,' he said. 'Shows his best side to you, he do.'

'He would to you, if you were as kind to him as I am,' said Micky, quick to put in a word. 'I'm always telling you Midge is a very nice little dog, Mr Fellin. He could be a great friend to you, and awfully good company, if you'd let him. Doesn't he look smart with his new collar?'

Fellin didn't say yes or no, but he privately thought it was a very fine collar, far too good for Midge. Still, that boy was cracked on the dog, so let him spend his money on it if he wanted to!

Micky missed Amanda that day. She disappeared till teatime, and then actually went off again, saying that Francie wasn't going home to tea till six o'clock, and she must get back and just finish one or two jobs with her.

Amanda and Francie had done a good job between them that day. The kitchen was quite finished and looked spotless and shining. The walls had been washed, the floor well scrubbed, and the sink was as good as new, though it had taken Francie more than an hour to get the dirt off.

'I won't half tell Rene what I think of her when she comes back,' grumbled the girl. 'She can't have done a thing for months.'

'Well, you know she must have been very ill,'

said Amanda. 'How you've made those taps shine, Francie!'

The sitting-room was not finished, but Francie generously remarked that it was twice as big as the kitchen and had three times as many things in it, and nobody could possibly clean it up properly in less than three days. So Amanda felt quite happy about not finishing it after all.

'I'll come back every day and help you,' she said to Francie. Francie looked a bit awkward.

'You'd better not do that,' she said, 'your ma mightn't like it. Anyway, it's my job, not yours. You just come and keep me company sometimes, and take Emily out like you wanted to.'

'You might come over lazy again,' said Amanda, grinning. 'No, I'll come, Francie. It's more fun to set to and work with you than to mess around doing nothing except jog Emily a bit. Let's get everything beautiful and surprise your mother and Rene and Ted. Micky said he'd help with the garden too.'

'I always thought you and your kind were stuck-up before,' Francie said unexpectedly. 'But you're not really. You're like your mother, I think, sort of friendly and kindly-like.'

I'll have to tell Mummy what nice things people think of her, thought Amanda to herself as she went home, tired out and yawning. Everyone seems to love her.

Podge's father came home on the Monday, and Podge, with a lot of good advice from the others, went to find him and tackle him about the Tupps. He badly wanted to do his job well. Micky and Amanda were both trying hard and getting good results. Podge felt he must too, whatever happened.

He found his father going through his letters in his study. He glanced up as Podge came in.

'What is it, Claude?' he said. 'Lost your bike again?'

'No, Dad,' said Podge. 'Er – I came to ask you – er – well, it's rather difficult to tell you – er . . .'

'Whatever is the matter with you?' Mr Paget said impatiently. 'It's not like you to stammer and stutter like this. What have you done?'

'Nothing,' said Podge. 'You see, it's like this – er . . .'

'If that's all you've got to say to me, you can go,' said Mr Paget. 'I've a great deal to do. If you've done anything wrong, out with it and tell me.'

'I haven't,' said Podge. And then it all came out with a rush. 'You see, Dad – it's about the Tupps. I know you are having them turned out next Saturday – and I wondered if anything could be done about it.'

His father stared at Podge as if he had

suddenly gone mad. 'What in the world is it to do with you?' he said. 'What do *you* know about the Tupps?'

'Mrs Tupp is terribly upset,' said Podge earnestly. 'Dad, if they are behind with their rent, let me pay for it and give them another chance!'

'You must be mad,' said Mr Paget, exasperated. 'I won't have you interfering like this. No, the Tupps are *not* behind with their rent. As if I should turn people out for that reason! You should know me better.'

Podge's heart suddenly felt lighter. He might have known his father wouldn't turn anyone out for that reason. He felt ashamed of himself for even thinking such a thing.

'Well, why are you turning them out then?' he asked. 'There are three children, Dad, two of them quite little.'

'If you want to know the real reason, I'll tell you,' said Mr Paget, looking hard at Podge. 'It's because the man is a bad lot, a hardened thief if ever there was one! It was he, for instance, who took your bicycle.'

Podge got a shock. He hadn't imagined the reason to be anything like that. He said nothing, but looked at his father. Mr Paget went on.

'He not only took your bicycle, but someone else's as well, and various tools from the fields, and a whole heap of scrap metal he found some-where, goodness knows why!' said Mr Paget. 'He even took a mower belonging to someone in the village, which had been sent from the maker's that day, brand new and shining.'

'Oh,' said Podge. 'I suppose Mr Philpot found all this out – and found the things too?'

'He did,' said Mr Paget. 'At first Philpot thought that elder boy of the Tupps had taken the things, but after a lot of questions and argu-ment, Tupp owned up to the thefts himself. If it hadn't been for Mrs Tupp breaking down most piteously, and begging for mercy for her hus-band, I and the other owners would have put the man into prison.' Podge listened in horror. What a wicked fellow Tupp must be!

'So, as I was Tupp's landlord, I said I would get him out of that cottage, which is mine, and make him leave the district,' said Mr Paget. 'I'm not having a fellow like that on my land. Now – do you feel as sorry for him as you did?'

'No,' said Podge. 'I don't. But I still feel sorry for that poor Mrs Tupp. After all, it isn't her fault, Dad.'

'Oh, no doubt she knew all about Tupp's thieving,' said his father. 'For all we know, she may have had a hand in it too. You needn't waste your pity on her. You'll see she'll find somewhere to go all right, before the week is out! Now, please don't interfere any more in my affairs, Podge. Go off with your friends, and let me get on with my work.'

Podge went out of the study, feeling rather small and upset. Fancy Tupp stealing all those things! And could Mrs Tupp be as bad as her husband? She didn't look it. She had a very nice face, really, quiet and patient and kind. It didn't look at all a bad face.

Podge went to find the other Put-Em-Rights. He felt sorry that his job had finished up like this – but there was nothing he could do now. He found all the others in the Rectory garden, talking hard. Clearly something else had cropped up – another job for somebody. Well, perhaps Podge could tackle that, and make up for trying to do a Put-Em-Right job that couldn't be done.

'Podge! Listen!' called Amanda, as he came up. 'We've got something else.'

'Just as well,' said Podge, gloomily. 'My job's finished. Nothing to be done.'

'What do you mean?' said Sally.

Podge told them everything. 'So it was Tupp who took your bike, and the other things Mr Philpot spoke about too!' said Micky. 'No wonder your father's turning him out.'

'Is this Put-Em-Right job a failure then?' asked Yolande, wide-eyed. 'I thought we

couldn't fail if we watched and prayed and worked.'

'Well, we haven't exactly failed,' said Sally. 'It's something we can't prevent from happening, because it's too big and impossible for us.'

'The Tramping Preacher said that nothing was impossible,' said Yolande. 'Not if God was behind us. I think we have failed.'

'You mean *I've* failed?' said Podge. 'Well, Yolande, it's a pity you didn't take this on yourself, then maybe you'd have done it better.'

Yolande was upset at Podge's impatient tone. But she wouldn't give in to him.

'No job should be too big for the Put-Em-Rights,' said the little girl stoutly. 'I believe something could be done still, even though it looks quite impossible.'

'Don't be silly, Yo,' said Amanda. 'If Podge can't do it, no one can. Podge is the oldest of any of us. It's just bad luck that he happened to fail because there were things we didn't know about it.'

'Anyway, if you feel so certain about it, take it on yourself,' said Micky. 'Ah, I thought that would make you look scared! It's all very well to go for other people when they fail, but you'd find it was just as hard, or harder, if you tried to do it yourself! So there!'

'And now let's tell Podge about our next job,'

said Sally. 'Shut up, all of you, and I'll tell Podge. It's quite an interesting task for the Put-Em-Rights.'

15

The Put-Em-Rights at work Again

'You know the family called Pepper, don't you?' began Sally. 'They sit at the back in church on Sundays. There's old Mrs Pepper, the grand-mother, and Alf Pepper, the father, and Mrs Pepper, and about six children going down like steps. Two of them are twins, boys about Bobby's age.'

'Yes, I've seen them,' said Podge. 'The twins are so alike I can never tell one from the other. They're little monkeys, too.'

'They are,' said Bobby, feelingly. They had often called rude names after him, especially since he had made such friends with the Rectory children and Podge and Yolande, and had turned up his nose at the village children.

'Well, an awful thing has happened to the family,' said Sally. 'Alf Pepper has been sent to prison! You know he hasn't been in the village for some time, he was away in the North some-where. And now the news is out that he borrowed someone's van one day and ran over an old woman. And he's been put into prison for it.'

'Goodness! How awful for the Pepper children!' said Yolande.

'Yes,' said Sally. 'And when people are put into prison they can't send any money to their wives, so the Pepper family are pretty hard up. The old grandmother is ill and so is the baby. I think it's a case for the Put-Em-Rights. We could make them feel that someone was sorry, and could help them over the worst, perhaps, till the father comes out of prison.'

'It must be pretty awful to know your father is in prison,' said Bobby, screwing up his nose. 'It must make the Pepper children feel awfully ashamed.'

'How did you get to hear about this?' asked Podge.

'Well, my mother went to see Mrs Pepper,' said Bobby, 'and she heard the grandmother talking about Alf Pepper. She asked Mrs Pepper about it when she came down, and Mrs Pepper wasn't very civil to her. But, anyway, Mother knew, and she told me, saying that I might do something, as I'm a Put-Em-Right.'

The others stared at him, annoyed. 'How did your mother know anything about the Put-Em-Rights?' demanded Sally. 'We said we wouldn't tell anybody.'

Bobby went red. How stupid of him to have let out that he had told his mother! 'Well,' he said at last, rather awkwardly, 'Mother likes to know everything, you see. She's only got me, and . . .'

'Don't make silly excuses,' said Podge. 'You know very well you don't tell your mother everything – and you only blabbed about us because you thought she'd like to know that you, her precious boy, were among the six Put-Em-Rights!' This was absolutely true, but Bobby was not going to admit it.

'You're disgusting,' said Sally. 'You can't be trusted! I shan't wear my button any more if you go round telling the whole village what P E R means.'

'And I don't think your mother ought to have listened to the talk between the grandmother and Mrs Pepper,' said Amanda.

'Don't let's quarrel,' said Yolande, anxiously.

'I'm sorry I told my mother about us,' said Bobby, afraid that the others would turn him out of the band. 'I didn't think. I haven't told anyone else at all. Honestly, I haven't.'

'We can't possibly help anyone if they know we're setting about putting things right,' said Sally. 'It might put their backs up against us. I think, Bobby, you ought to take on this job yourself. The Peppers wouldn't like any of us knowing about Alf being in prison, and you can say that your mother told you.'

Bobby didn't in the least want the job. But he thought he had better say he would take it on and try to get back into the others' good books. So he nodded.

'All right. I'll have a shot at it. I could take some soup or something to the old lady. And I could dig a bit of Mrs Pepper's garden for her. Since her husband has been away, I expect there has been no one to do it.'

'I dare say my mother would take Mrs Pepper on for a few jobs in the house,' said Podge. 'That would help a bit in the money line. And those twins could easily do a bit of fruit-picking now. My father wants the plums picked.'

'I'll tell them,' said Bobby, seeing himself suddenly as a perfect saint, bringing light and help to a sad household. 'I'll get my mother to make the soup or something today.'

Amanda soon disappeared, rushing off to help Francie with the house. Yolande wished she could go with her, but Amanda seemed to think it was her job and nobody else's. She and Francie had entirely finished the sitting-room and kitchen now, and were starting on the bedrooms. Francie knew how to work, in spite of her laziness, and had taught Amanda all kinds of things about cleaning a house thoroughly.

Alice, the Rectory daily help, had been amused at some of Amanda's questions lately. 'What's the best polish to use for brass? What's the best thing to use for red tiles, not white ones? How do you get a kettle clean inside when it's all caked up?'

'Well, I never – you'll be a proper little house-wife one day after all!' said Alice. 'And you'll be giving me a surprise, too – making your bed, or dusting your room or something!'

Yolande watched Amanda disappearing down the drive. She was bitterly disappointed that Podge seemed to have failed in his Put-Em-Right job. She still thought something could have been done, and she remembered how Micky had laughed at her, and told her to do it herself, if she felt like that!

155

I've a good mind to wander down to the village, and talk to the Tupp children, thought Yolande suddenly. I might be able to help in some way, you never know.

So off she went, all by herself. She came to the Tupps' lane and went down it. Soon she arrived at a gate and she climbed up on it. It swung open, and the little girl began to swing to and fro, to and fro.

Presently two little girls came along the lane. They stared at Yolande. They had bright red hair, curly and coarse. Their faces were freckled.

'Have a swing?' said Yolande.

One little girl got on to the gate and swung herself. 'This is our gate,' she said to Yolande. 'We swing here.'

'Oh,' said Yolande. 'I didn't know. Is it your field, then?'

'No,' said the other little girl. 'But it's our gate. We say it's our gate. We live down there, at the end cottage.'

Yolande felt that they must be the Tupps and she was pleased.

'What are your names?' she asked.

'I'm Meryl Tupp and she's Linda Tupp,' said Meryl and got up on the gate too. 'This gate is my horse, see? And this gatepost is my horse's head.'

'We're going on Saturday,' said Linda. 'We

shan't have this gate any more then. You can have it if you like.'

'Thank you,' said Yolande. 'Why are you going, Linda?'

'Don't know,' said Linda.

'Because Will was naughty,' said Meryl, and swung herself again.

'Who's Will?' said Yolande.

'Our big brother,' said Meryl. 'He's a bad boy. Dad says so. He shouted at him one night and Will screamed. He woke us up. He's a bad, bad boy.'

'Why is he bad?' asked Yolande, puzzled.

The little girls didn't know. They only knew that Will was bad, and had been scolded.

'Here's Will now,' said Linda, and she pointed up the lane. Yolande saw a big boy coming along, with red hair, sandy eyebrows and freckles all over his face. He had a furtive, deceitful look, and she didn't like him. She slipped down from the gate and hid in the hedge, in case he told her to get off the gate that belonged to Linda and Meryl.

Will didn't see Yolande. He slouched past his two sisters and went into a little broken-down shed, his hands in his pockets. He soon came out again.

'That's Will's hidy-hole,' Meryl said to Yolande. 'Come and see what he's put there.'

The three of them went into the little old shed. There were sacks in one corner, which Meryl pulled away. Underneath was a gleaming pocket knife. As soon as she saw it Yolande pounced on it.

'Why, it's Podge's knife – my cousin's knife,' she said to the two surprised little girls. 'He lost it some days ago. Your brother ought to have taken it to the police if he had found it. He shouldn't hide it away.'

'You put it back,' said Meryl, looking round as if afraid that someone might hear. 'Put it back. It's Will's and this is his hidy-hole. He once slapped me and Linda for peeping.'

'I'm not going to put it back,' said Yolande. 'I'm going to take it to your mother and explain that it's my cousin's knife, and tell her I'm giving it back to him.'

Halfway down the lane she remembered the fierce Mr Tupp and stopped.

'Where's your father?' she asked Meryl and Linda, who were trotting beside her.

'Gone off in the bus,' said Meryl. So Yolande went on, feeling a bit safer. She would not have liked to speak to Mr Tupp at all.

She came to the Tupps' house. Mrs Tupp was at the door, shaking a mat. She called to Meryl and Linda.

'You come along in now. I've been looking for you.'

'Ma! This girl's found something our Will hid!' cried Meryl. 'She took it! Our Will won't like that!'

Mrs Tupp looked sharply at Yolande, and her face was worried and unhappy. 'What do you mean?' she said sharply to Meryl. Then she spoke to Yolande. 'Come in a minute and tell me, will you?'

Yolande went in and Mrs Tupp shut the door

and sat down at the table. Yolande showed her
the knife, and told her how Will had come by,
had gone into the shed, and had left the pocket
knife there.

'And, you see, it's my cousin's knife, Podge's,'
she said. 'He lost it a little while ago. It's got
his name on, look.'

She showed Mrs Tupp the knife, and there,
engraved boldly on it, was Podge's name,
Claude Paget.

'Claude Paget!' said Mrs Tupp, and suddenly she began to cry very softly. Yolande had never seen a grown-up cry before, and she was very much upset.

'What's the matter?' she said to Mrs Tupp. 'Do tell me what's the matter!'

'I can't tell a little girl like you,' said Mrs Tupp. 'You wouldn't understand. But I do beg of you not to tell anyone about this, not anyone at all!'

16

Yolande
runs Away

Yolande held Podge's pocket knife tightly, and felt her knees shaking a little, as they always did when she was afraid. Suppose Mr Tupp came back soon? Suppose he shouted at her as he had shouted at Podge.

Yolande didn't want to stay in the Tupps' hot little kitchen one moment longer. She wanted to run away. Yolande often wanted to run away from things. She had run away from hundreds already in her short life – spiders, mice, scoldings, quarrels, even parties when she felt shy!

But this was worse than anything she had ever been afraid of before. There was poor Mrs Tupp, crying quietly to herself, the two little girls staring wide-eyed – and then suddenly into the room came the big boy who had hidden the pocket knife in the shed! Yolande trembled.

The boy caught sight of the knife and made an angry noise. 'Mine!' he said.

'It isn't, oh, it isn't,' said Yolande, and held on to it more tightly than ever.

'It's not yours, Will,' said Mrs Tupp, drying her eyes and speaking in a low, firm voice. 'You know it's not. What did your father tell you off for the other night, and what did you promise him? Didn't he scold you for taking things that didn't belong to you? Didn't you promise him you'd never take bicycles or anything again? Do you want to be told off again?'

'No, Ma,' said Will and blinked his pale blue eyes. 'But that's my knife. That girl found it in my shed.'

'Oh, Will! You haven't been hiding things there again, have you?' cried Mrs Tupp. Will stood on one foot and looked sulky: he didn't take his eyes off the shining pocket knife.

Yolande was so astonished at what she heard that she forgot her fears. 'But, Mrs Tupp,' she said, speaking loudly, 'I thought it was Mr Tupp that stole the bicycle and things!'

Mrs Tupp jumped and looked frightened. She looked hard at Yolande. 'What do you know about things?' she demanded. 'How do you know anything about Mr Tupp and what he does? Answer me that!'

Yolande was taken aback at the sudden sharp tone. 'Well,' she said at last, 'well, you see, my cousin, Claude Paget, heard it from his father. We know you're being turned out because Mr Tupp took things that didn't belong to him.

Does Will steal things, too, then? How awful for you!'

Mrs Tupp said nothing for a moment. Then she turned to her three listening children. 'Go on out for a minute,' she said. 'And shut the door. Go on, now.'

The big lad and the little girls went out, looking surprised. Mrs Tupp turned to Yolande. 'Now, see here,' she said earnestly, 'will you promise me not to tell anyone that Will took that knife? Don't you breathe a word about it!'

'But I must give it back to Podge, and he'll want to know all about it,' said Yolande. 'I think Will was bad not to take it to the police station when he found it.'

'Will's not bad,' said Mrs Tupp. 'He's not. He's just a poor, unlucky fellow, that's all. When he was a baby he fell out of his pram and cracked his head on the stone yard. And ever since he's not been as well as other children. See? He doesn't understand things. He's like a jackdaw: when he sees anything shining bright, he takes it – it may be a bicycle or a bright pocket knife, like the one you've got, or just a bit of scrap metal. He don't mind what it is, if it shines.'

Yolande listened in astonishment. Mrs Tupp went on, speaking so earnestly that the little girl never in all her life forgot one word of what the unhappy woman said.

'One day our Will may be better – if he stays at home here with me. I understand him, I do. I know what he does isn't done because he's bad; it's only because he has a fancy for shining things. He's always been like that. But if the police know that our Will is the one that's been taking things, they'll make him go away from me, they'll put him into some home far away, they'll tell him he's bad, and make him think he is. And he'll be that unhappy.'

'Oh, Mrs Tupp, I'm so sorry,' said Yolande, with tears in her eyes. 'Poor, poor Will! How awful that he fell out of his pram like that! But perhaps if a doctor saw him, he could be put right. My daddy's a doctor. Let me tell him.'

'They'll take my Will away if they know he picks up anything shiny that takes his eyes,' said Mrs Tupp obstinately. 'That's what we're afraid of. I love poor Will. It would break my heart if anything happened to him. John, that's my husband, he loves him too.'

Yolande thought Will was lucky to have two people loving him so much, as he didn't seem to her to be in the least lovable. A thought came to her suddenly.

'Oh, Mrs Tupp! Is that why Mr Tupp said *he* took the things – so as to shield poor Will, and not have him taken away?'

'Don't you let on to anybody!' begged Mrs

Tupp, looking round as if the whole village were listening. 'I shouldn't have let you know. But you finding that knife upset me, like. You be a nice kind girl and don't say anything to anybody. Mr Tupp and I, we'll do anything rather than have our Will taken away and told he's bad. Yes, we'd rather go to prison than that!'

'But Mrs Tupp, you're being turned out on Saturday because of this,' said Yolande, remembering. 'And won't Mr Tupp find it difficult to get a job now?'

Before Mrs Tupp could answer, the kitchen door opened and Mr Tupp came in. He looked at Yolande in surprise, not knowing who she was. Yolande sat as if she was turned into stone. She was so frightened that she could neither speak nor move.

'Who's this?' said Mr Tupp.

Yolande suddenly found her feet. Before Mrs Tupp could say who she was, she shot by the surprised Mr Tupp and ran out of the kitchen and up the lane faster than she had ever run in her life before. How she ran! Poor Yolande, she was sure that if she didn't put at least a mile between her and Mr Tupp he would catch her and shake her till her teeth rattled!

She ran and she ran, panting and puffing, her heart beating and thumping. She turned a corner and was almost run over by Podge on his

bicycle! He just swerved aside in time. Yolande's legs gave way beneath her and she sat down suddenly on a patch of grass. Then the excitement and hard running made her feel peculiar and she opened her mouth and howled!

Podge leaped off his bicycle at once and ran to his little cousin. 'You're not hurt, are you?' he said anxiously, putting his arms round her. 'What's up, Yo?'

Yolande howled dismally for a minute or two and then, feeling less exhausted, and much comforted by the anxious Podge, she became quieter and rubbed her wet eyes with her hands. Podge saw something in one of them and suddenly gave an exclamation.

'My lost pocket knife! Where did you find it, Yo? And what on earth were you coming along at sixty miles an hour for?'

Yolande looked at him. 'I don't think I ought to tell what has happened to me this afternoon,' she said. 'Mrs Tupp asked me not to say anything.'

'Mrs *Tupp*! Have you been down there?' said Podge, amazed. 'What were you doing there?'

'Mrs Tupp asked me not to tell anyone,' said Yolande, simply longing to pour everything out to Podge.

'Did you promise not to?' said Podge. 'You shouldn't promise a thing like that, because you know we all said we would tell the band everything. We can't do things on our own, in case we do them wrong.'

'Oh,' said Yolande. 'Well – no – I didn't promise Mrs Tupp I wouldn't tell. I – I ran away before I promised. I was an awful coward, Podge. I ran and I ran.'

'Tell me all about it,' said Podge. So the two of them sat down on the bank by the wayside and Yolande told her story.

Podge listened in the greatest interest and surprise. He could hardly believe that Yolande had found out so much about the Tupps.

'This alters everything,' he said. 'This means that maybe we can still do something to put things right for the poor Tupps. But we'll have to bring in one or two grown-ups, there's no doubt about that.'

'So – this job isn't finished – it isn't a failure?' said Yolande, with her eyes shining. 'I didn't think it could be really, Podge, because you've no idea how hard I prayed about it last night.'

'You're rather a pet,' said Podge, and gave his small cousin a sudden hug. 'The smallest and the least brave – and yet you bearded the Tupps in their den, found out what I didn't find, and gave us the key to the problem. Come on, we must tell the others at once.'

But they couldn't tell them immediately because Bobby wasn't there and Amanda was once more at the cottage with Francie. So they had to wait till the evening, when everyone gathered to report the progress made on the various jobs in hand.

Micky had nothing to report. Amanda merely reported more progress with the cleaning of the house, and said that she had washed and ironed ever so many baby clothes and they did look nice. Bobby hadn't been able to get on with his job because his mother hadn't finished making the soup for the old grandmother. So it was left to Yolande and Podge to provide the real news.

Everyone was amazed at what Yolande had discovered. 'You did jolly well,' said Mick admiringly. 'All on your own too! I think this had better be her turn at doing a job, don't you, Podge? She can't tackle anything else at present. This is Yo's own Put-Em-Right work.'

'Oh, fancy!' said Yolande, her cheeks glowing. 'I was simply terrified of tackling any job – and now I'm right in the middle of one and I like it. But I wish I hadn't run away.'

'Anyone would run away from Mr Tupp if they thought he was going to be in a temper,' Podge said comfortingly. 'Well, Yo, I think the next thing for you to do is to talk to your father when he comes back from his holiday. He's coming to Four Towers with your mother this week, isn't he? You tell him about Will Tupp then, and see what he says. Maybe he will say something can be done for the boy, without taking him away from home.'

'Oh, yes!' said Amanda. 'Your father is a brain-doctor, isn't he? He knows all about brain illnesses, so he might be able to cure Will. Yolande, what a wonderful Put-Em-Right you'll be if that happens!'

'And your father can talk to mine, and maybe the Tupps won't be turned out after all!' said Podge. 'Good old Yo!'

17

Bobby and
the Peppers

The next day Bobby set about his own particular Put-Em-Right job. He meant to do it well. He really fancied himself as someone bringing help and comfort to a stricken household. He only wished it didn't contain those rude twins. Still, that couldn't be helped.

Bobby's mother was pleased that Bobby had been chosen to help the Peppers. She didn't like Mrs Pepper, whom she thought was a very uncivil, disobliging woman. She did not realise that it was her own foolishly haughty manner that made the Peppers rude to her. It pleased her that misfortune and disgrace had come to the Peppers, and that she and her Bobby could act like saints to them.

'Now, here's a big jug of soup for the old lady,' said Mrs Jones to Bobby the next morning. 'And here's a cake I've baked. It means we'll have to go without one this week, but never mind; think how good it is to help others in misfortune! And you tell Mrs Pepper I'll get her more ironing if she needs the money.'

Bobby set off, carrying the soup carefully, covered over with a cloth. He had the cake in a basket. Secretly, he thought it was a waste of a cake, and he resented having to go without it himself. It wouldn't go far among that big family of Peppers! He walked up the little path to the Peppers' front door, rehearsing the kindly speech he meant to make. But one of the Pepper children jogged his arm, upsetting a little of the soup, which made him cross.

'Don't do that!' he said sharply. 'Where are your manners?'

'Haven't got any!' the Pepper child answered, and nudged him again. 'We aren't all Mamma's good little boy, like you!'

Slop went the soup again. 'Look here,' said Bobby, exasperated, 'this is jolly good soup I'm bringing for your grandmother!'

The Pepper child stared in surprise and jogged no more, but accompanied Bobby to the front door. He rang the bell, but there was no answer.

'You go round the back,' said the Pepper child. 'Ma's out in the garden, hanging out the clothes, I expect.'

'I'm not used to going to back doors,' Bobby said with a high-and-mighty air.

'Well, stand here all the morning, then,' said the Pepper child, grinning, and disappeared round the back. He told his mother that Bobby Jones, old 'Stuck-Up Jones', was at the front door, and wouldn't go round to the back because he wasn't used to that! Mrs Pepper laughed.

'Let him stand at the front door then,' she said, and went on hanging up the sheets.

'That's what I told him,' said the Pepper child, and went back to the front garden where he leaned against the fence and watched Bobby standing patiently at the front door. He gave Bobby plenty of advice.

'Knock *and* ring,' he said. Bobby took no

notice, but stood like a martyr, waiting.

The Pepper boy had far too much to say and enjoyed saying it. It was nice to get back at 'Stuck-Up Jones' for the many irritations he had caused the Peppers and the other village children. They were a friendly, companionable lot, and resented Bobby's disdain of them. Bobby tried not to listen.

'Soup's getting cold, isn't it?' said the Pepper child. Bobby looked into the jug. Blow! It was getting cold. There was no help for it but to go round the back after all and see if anyone was there!

So round the back he went, and walked straight into old Mrs Pepper, the grandmother. She was surprised to see Bobby Jones, and said so.

'I've brought you some soup, Mrs Pepper,' said Bobby, in his most kindly and polite tones. 'I'm very, very sorry for your trouble. My mother and I thought you might like to know that we are thinking about you, and would like to help you in every way.'

Mrs Pepper was deaf and hardly caught a word but 'soup'.

'What's the soup for?' she said, and she called her daughter-in-law to her. 'Hey, Lucy, here's a boy with soup. What's he doing bringing soup here? Has he got the wrong address?'

'And I've got a cake for you too,' went on Bobby, rather nervously. 'It's – it's always a help, don't you think, when you are in trouble, to have a little kindness from neighbours?'

'What are you talking about?' said Mrs Pepper, the mother. 'Who's in trouble, I should like to know? And what's it to do with you, anyway?'

'Er – Mum told me about poor Alf,' said Bobby.

Mrs Pepper gave a sudden exclamation. 'That mother of yours! How dare she sit in my kitchen and listen to things she's got no right to hear? Who's she to give herself such airs? Sending you round here with soft words and soup! I'll soup you!'

And, to Bobby's intense horror, she snatched the jug of lukewarm soup and poured it over him! The Pepper twins, who had just come in, screamed with delight to see poor Bobby dripping with greasy soup.

'Look at him! Stuck-Up Jones! Lick it off, Stuck-Up, lick it off!'

The Peppers' dog smelled the soup and came running up. It stood up on its hind legs and began to lick Bobby with enjoyment. Bobby was almost in tears. He pushed the dog away.

'If this is all your return for kindness, you ought to be ashamed of yourselves!' he shouted.

'Kindness? What kindness?' said Mrs Pepper sharply. 'If there had been any real kindness about you or your mother, I'd be the first to welcome you, and say thank you. But you're hypocrites, the pair of you. You're glad if trouble comes to us. You want to come and gloat, don't you? You want to play the little saint and give us charity, and expect us to lick your boots!'

'Woof,' said the dog, enjoying himself.

'Look at Tinker,' said a Pepper child. 'He hasn't had such a meal for ages! Give him the cake, old Stuck-Up.'

But Bobby was going to hang on to the cake for all he was worth! He wasn't going to give up his teatime cake now, for any Pepper person or dog! He rubbed the soup out of his eyes, clutched his basket firmly and turned to go.

'Here,' said Mrs Pepper, suddenly ashamed of what she had done. 'You come in and let me clean you up a bit, see? I was a bit hasty, but you riled me proper, you did, with your namby-pamby airs, looking down your nose at us all the time!'

She took Bobby into her kitchen and got off as much soup as she could, Tinker helping with all his might. Bobby was sullen and resentful. How could you help people when they yelled at you and threw soup all over you?

'There you are,' said Mrs Pepper. 'Now you go home and tell that mother of yours if she comes snooping round here again, hearing things she's not meant to hear, I'll throw soup over her, too. And, what's more, I won't clean her up afterwards!'

Bobby went home, but he did not tell his mother all that Mrs Pepper had said. He was smarting under a sense of failure. He felt he hadn't gone about things the right way. Mrs Pepper was right when she said he had gone there looking down his nose at them. He hadn't gone in a really kindly, friendly spirit: he had gone feeling rather glad that bad luck had come to the Peppers, and he had secretly hoped they would bow and scrape to him for his unexpected gifts.

Mrs Jones was furious when she saw Bobby's spoilt clothes. 'The ungrateful wretches!' she cried. 'I shall go round to Mrs Pepper myself and tell that woman what I think of her! And I'll tell the whole village about her husband being in prison now, so I will! I wasn't going to say a word, being down right sorry for them – but they don't deserve any consideration at all!'

'No, Mum, don't do anything like that,' said Bobby, alarmed. 'Please don't. I'm sure the Put-Em-Rights wouldn't like it. And, whatever you do, don't go and quarrel with Mrs Pepper. I shall have to try again somehow, and you'll make things awfully difficult for me. Please don't. I don't know what Micky and Amanda and Podge and Yolande would think of me if you go and make a row. I'd probably never be asked there again.'

Mrs Jones didn't want Bobby to be thrown out of the Put-Em-Rights, nor did she want them to stop asking Bobby to their houses. It was something she could boast of, and make the other mothers jealous about. Her Bobby, and his fine friends, and the teas he had at Four Towers, and what a lot the Rector and his wife thought of him. No, it wouldn't do to hurt Bobby's friendship with the other children.

But I shall put round the village that that Alf Pepper is in prison! she thought viciously. And I'll tell everyone how my Bobby belongs to the Put-Em-Rights – silly name they've chosen – and how he went to the Peppers to help and they threw soup over him, poor boy. Yes, I'll show them up properly.

So, although Mrs Jones did not go to the Peppers and 'tick them off' as she wanted to, she did spread the evil news, telling everyone that Alf Pepper was in prison and serve him right – and serve the Pepper family right, too, being in disgrace and all – the way they treated her Bobby when he went to help them and comfort them in their trouble.

Soon the whole village knew about the six Put-Em-Rights. The village boys were delighted

with the news, and Bobby had a very bad time as he went about.

'Put me right!' yelled one of the boys as Bobby passed. 'Won't you put me right? I told a story yesterday, and I want to be put right!'

'I've gone all wrong!' shouted a girl. 'My sock's got a hole in. Put it right, Bobby Jones, put it right.'

> 'Poor old Bobby Put-Em-Right,
> Wasn't he a dreadful sight,
> Soo-oo-oup!'

– yelled a chorus of boys, making up the silly rhyme on the spur of the moment, and bringing in the *soup* with much gusto. Bobby's face burned red and he felt very miserable and unhappy. His mother shouldn't have told about the Put-Em-Rights.

It's awful, thought Bobby to himself. No one is pointing their fingers at the Pepper children, whose father is in prison; but they're all, all of them, jeering at me. It isn't fair! I hate them all!

18

Good News
for the Tupps

The Put-Em-Rights were displeased when they heard what had happened to Bobby. He made out as good a case for himself as he could, but Podge saw the weak spot at once.

'You thought too much of yourself and the soup and the cake, and not enough of the Peppers themselves,' he said. 'That was where you failed, Bobby.'

'And look here, Bobby, have you been telling everyone about us, and saying we are the Put-Em-Rights?' said Amanda. 'A village boy yelled "Put-Em-Right" after me today – not nastily, but sort of amused.'

'No, I haven't said anything to anyone except my mother,' said Bobby, embarrassed, for he guessed his mother had told everyone about the Put-Em-Rights and how he, Bobby, was only doing his duty as a P E R when he went to the Peppers.

'Well, someone's blabbed about us,' said Podge, disgusted.

'It's too bad,' said Sally. 'It makes things so difficult for us. I always thought it was a silly name, anyhow; and now other people know it, we shall be laughed at.'

'Well, that won't hurt us, I suppose,' said Micky. 'Bobby, you'll have to go on with this Put-Em-Right job. Won't he, everyone?'

'Yes,' said Sally. 'It will be more difficult now, Bobby, because you started off the wrong way. Try the right way next time.'

'But I can't go to the Peppers any more!' said poor Bobby in horror. 'I simply can't. I've made an absolute mess of it. I suppose I did do it the wrong way, but I certainly can't do it the right way now.'

'Well, you've got to try,' decided Podge. 'Go and say you are sorry to have put their backs up, and set to work in their garden or something, to show them you mean it.'

'The Pepper children will laugh at me like anything,' said Bobby. 'I can't. I really can't.'

'Well, you're not a Put-Em-Right, then,' said Amanda. There was a pause. Bobby sat miserably silent.

'Would you like to resign from the band?' Sally asked coldly.

'No,' Bobby answered, thinking how upset his mother would be if he no longer went about with the Rectory and Four Towers children. 'I'll

– I'll try again. But I do think I've got the very hardest thing to do of anybody!'

'Well, you've made it hard for yourself,' said Sally severely. Yolande looked at the miserable Bobby.

'Don't be too hard on poor Bobby,' she said to Sally. 'You always sound so stern, Sally.'

'Wait till Sally gets a job to do,' said Podge. 'She may find that she can't settle it as easily as she thinks. She may make a mess of it like Bobby, or think it's impossible like I did! You wait, Sally! It's your turn next.'

'I shan't be silly about it, I shall be sensible,' said Sally. 'I'm used to managing quite difficult things at school: you can't be head of your form, and a big form too, without learning how to tackle all kinds of problems in the right way. A little common sense solves most things.'

'Isn't Sally wonderful?' said Micky lazily. 'She ought to be prime minister.'

'Don't be funny,' said Sally, offended. She never could learn to laugh when she was teased.

'My father and mother are coming back tomorrow,' said Yolande. 'I've got to talk to Daddy then, haven't I, Podge?'

'Yes. I'll come and hold your hand if you think you're afraid of facing your own father!' said Podge.

'I'm not. But I think it would be a help if

you came, all the same, Podge,' said Yolande. 'Daddy might listen to you more than to me. You're older. Besides, it was your Put-Em-Right job to begin with, too, wasn't it?'

'It was,' agreed Podge. 'All right, I'll come.'

So the next day, when Yolande's father and mother came to Four Towers, brown from their holiday, Yolande said she had something to discuss with him. Her father was amused at her solemn face.

'Something to discuss?' he said. 'Well, come along then. Is it some secret? Oh, is Podge coming too? All right, we'll go into the garden.'

In the garden, cuddled up to her father, Yolande told the whole story of the Tupps. Podge

helped her, and Dr Paget listened with great interest.

'Well, you seem to have poked your noses into the Tupps' affairs all right!' he said. 'I must have a word with Dick about this. You say he is going to turn the Tupps out on Saturday, Podge? Well, there's no time to be lost.'

He went off to find his brother, Podge's father, straight away. Yolande let out an enormous sigh of relief. 'It's nice being a Put-Em-Right, but it sort of helps when a grown-up takes charge, doesn't it?' she said to Podge. 'Do you think things will be all right now?'

'We'll see,' said Podge. 'Your father and mine will have a good old talk, I expect. Mine will be surprised when he hears it wasn't old Tupp who took the things, but poor Will!'

He certainly was surprised. He could hardly believe his ears when his doctor brother told him what Yolande and Podge had said. 'Well, of course, this alters matters considerably,' he said. 'What an extraordinary thing! Fancy these children interfering like this.'

'Well, they seem to have interfered to good purpose this time,' said his brother. 'I think the best thing for me to do is to go down and see Mrs Tupp, and examine that boy Will. Maybe he can be put right. His fancy for bright things, and his craving for them, isn't uncommon if his brain was injured in babyhood. As the children say, he isn't bad: I believe something might be done for him.'

'Well, tell Mrs Tupp I certainly shan't turn her out, now I know the truth,' said Mr Paget. 'I'm sorry about the whole thing. But Tupp swore he had taken the things himself, and I had no way of knowing that he was shielding that poor boy of his.'

Podge and Yolande were delighted when Mr Paget told them he had no intention now of turning out the Tupps on Saturday. Yolande flew to him and gave him a hug like a bear. He set down the excited little girl and smiled.

'Well, for a scared little girl like you, afraid of so many things, you did very well to solve the mystery of the Tupps and put things right for them!' he said. 'But we mustn't hope too much for Will, in case nothing can be done. However, your father will do his very best, Yolande, so we can safely leave things to him.'

Mrs Tupp was surprised and a little frightened when a big car drew up outside her house that day, and a kindly, dark-eyed man came up to the front door. She was really scared when he began to talk about Will.

But gradually hope came into her heart as she heard, first, that there was no fear of her being turned out on Saturday, and secondly, that Mr

Paget knew Mr Tupp was not to blame for the thefts, and was willing to give him a job.

'Oh, thank you more than I can say!' she said. 'But – but – don't do anything to poor Will, don't take him away.'

'Now listen, Mrs Tupp,' said Dr Paget, in his deep, kindly voice, 'I believe that Will may be made better – I really do believe this – and I am sure you would be the last person to prevent him from being made well. That injury he had when he was young has kept him back all his life; but nowadays these things can be put right. If you will let me have Will in my hospital for a little while – two or three weeks, maybe – so that I can watch him and make up my mind about him, it is possible that I may be able to do something that will make an ordinary boy of him, instead of a poor, bewildered child whose muddled brain makes him take anything bright and shining he sees!'

Mrs Tupp listened to Dr Paget and wiped her eyes. Her heart warmed to this doctor with his dark, kind eyes.

'Oh, Doctor,' she said, 'you do what you think best. I know you'll take care of my Will – and you'll let me have him back if you can't do anything to help him. You do promise me that, don't you? Will wants someone to love him and understand him. He'll turn into a real bad boy if he doesn't have someone to love him.'

'I know that,' said Dr Paget. 'Of course you shall have him back if I can't make him better. I'll come and fetch him tomorrow, Mrs Tupp. Now, don't worry. I believe there is a very good chance of putting him right. You'll be proud of him!'

Mrs Tupp was quite overcome with all her unexpected good luck: not to be turned out, and John to have his job back, and maybe Will put right! It seemed wonderful to her, and she called Meryl and Linda in to give them a treat of bread and treacle. Will got a slice too, and sat contentedly eating it, pleased at the unexpectedly happy face of his mother.

The Put-Em-Rights were filled with joy when they heard what had happened: Yolande's small face was radiant.

'My dad's a Put-Em-Right, too,' she said. 'He's always putting people right, isn't he? Oh, won't it be marvellous if Will can be put right? I do really feel we've managed to get something done!'

'Well, don't forget the grown-ups came in at the last,' said Micky. 'Without them we couldn't have finished off the job at all. It needed your father to see to Will, and your uncle to forgive the Tupps.'

'Will's going tomorrow,' said Podge. 'I hope he won't be too miserable in hospital. He'll probably try to grab all the shining scissors and things he sees!'

Everyone was pleased that what had seemed an impossible task should have turned out so well. Privately, Micky wished his job was turning out better, and as for Bobby, he groaned inwardly when he thought of how he had to tackle the Peppers again. It was a real ordeal to him now to go through the village, with the boys shouting after him.

Amanda was getting on very well indeed with her job. She and Francie had spent the whole week slaving in the little cottage, and they had almost finished it. Emily looked better than she had done for months, for she had regular airings, was well looked after, and enjoyed the company of the two girls.

'We're starting on the garden next week, Micky,' said Amanda. 'Will you come and help too? You said you would.'

'I'll come too,' said Podge. He didn't like gardening but he thought he had better give a hand; Podge was feeling rather ashamed of himself that day. His father had called him into his study and spoken sternly to him.

'I suppose you realise, Claude, that a lot of the Tupps' trouble was due to you?' he said. 'It was you who carelessly left your bicycle in that field and didn't bother to go back for it, so that poor Will found it and took it, seeing it shining there?'

'Yes,' said Podge, going red.

'And because of that I had the police in, and the bicycle was traced; and Mr Tupp said he had taken it, in order to shield that poor boy of his,' went on his father. 'It was because of your carelessness and irresponsibility that Mr Tupp lost his job and I threatened to turn them out. I know that as it is, thanks mainly to little Yolande, things are turning out better; but they might not have done so.'

'No,' agreed Podge, feeling dismal.

'You wouldn't have liked to think that that

family was without a home, and the man without a job, merely because you were careless and put temptation in the way of a wretched lad, would you?' said his father sternly. 'Remember this, Claude, that the more money and possessions and power we have, the more responsible and thoughtful we should be. You are not very high in my estimation at the moment. See if you can turn over a new leaf and learn to be sensible and trustworthy. Then maybe one day you'll do something for the world.'

'Yes. I will,' said Podge. And he meant it.

19

Strange News for Bobby

Will was taken off to the hospital. He didn't really seem to mind going at all. There would be no definite news about him for a while, but Dr Paget had promised to let the children know when he had made up his mind about Will.

Micky was still going on with his daily job of making Midge into a nice little dog and trying to persuade Fellin to think so too. But it seemed as if he was failing dismally.

Amanda was going to begin on the garden at Mrs Potts's cottage now. She and Francie were very good friends indeed, and Francie sincerely admired the way Amanda had tackled the house-work, not giving up or shirking once.

'I'd always heard you were a lazy one,' she told Amanda. 'Alice told my mother you wouldn't lift a finger to help your mother, no, not if she was tired out. But I don't believe that now. No one who works like you've worked in Rene's cottage could be lazy. I bet you help your mother all you can.'

Amanda was rather silent after these remarks. How horrid of Alice to say a thing like that! But after all – it was true. Alice had often scolded her for letting her mother do everything. 'You might at least do the flowers for her!' she had often said. Or, 'Why don't you take those parish magazines round for your mother today? She's real tired.'

It's funny, thought Amanda. Here I am, working hard for Rene, whom I hardly know – just to show Francie I'm not lazy – when I really am a very lazy person indeed. It's not very nice to think I can work hard just to make Francie think I can, when at home I don't do a thing for my own mother, that I love. Well – when I've finished this Put-Em-Right job, I'll offer to do lots of jobs at home. I know how to now. I could help Mummy a lot.

Bobby had a very bad time the next week. He kept putting off going to the Peppers again. He stayed at home a lot so that he wouldn't have to go out and be shouted at by the village children. He couldn't seem to make up his mind to go to the Peppers, say he was sorry he had put their backs up, and set to work in their garden to show his good intentions. He simply could not do it.

I'm feeble, he thought. I'm a bad Put-Em-Right. I'm afraid. I'm as bad as little Yolande.

Yet she wouldn't give up, and it was really because of her that the Tupp business was put right.

At last Bobby made up his mind to go to the Peppers. Rather shaky at the knees, he set out, and this time he carried nothing with him. He passed the house once, not daring to go in. Then, taking the plunge, he shot in at the gate. This time he did not go ringing and knocking at the front door. He went straight round to the back. The kitchen door was open, and inside he could see Mrs Pepper beating something in a basin. She glanced up and saw him.

'Mrs Pepper,' began Bobby desperately, 'I've come to say I'm sorry for putting your back up the other day. I acted in a silly way, I know. Please can I work in your garden for you a bit, to show you I really do want to do something?'

Mrs Pepper was astonished. She went on beating the egg for a little while, thinking. The old granny called out to her, 'Why, there's that boy who brought the soup the other day. What's he want, Lucy?'

'He says he's sorry he acted silly the other day, and can he work in the garden to make up?' shouted Mrs Pepper.

'Ah. So them Joneses has come to their senses,' said the old woman. 'Well, you let him work in the garden, Lucy. It can do with some hoeing and weeding. Them twins is too lazy to do a thing, and what Alf will say when he comes back, I don't know!'

So Bobby was set to work in the garden. He didn't know where the older Pepper children were, but he was extremely glad they were not there. Only the two youngest were there, and they were not big enough to be rude.

But soon Bobby got a shock. The twins came running down the back way to the kitchen door, shouting, 'Ma! Ma!' And, to Bobby's horror, they poured out to their infuriated mother something they had heard in the village.

'Miss Brown says our pa's in prison, Ma! You never told us! Is he in prison? Miss Brown said Mrs Jones told her – that Stuck-Up Jones boy's mother!'

Mrs Pepper wiped her hands on her apron. 'That woman!' she said. 'What lies she does spread about! No, your father's not in prison, nor likely to be, either. He's coming home tomorrow, if he can get off his job.'

Trembling with rage, Mrs Pepper went out to Bobby, who was standing horrified with his hoe. So his mother had spread abroad the titbit about Alf Pepper. How could she! And now Mrs Pepper knew, and would take it out of him!

Mrs Pepper advanced towards him, but she did not cuff him or order him off. She took him

by the arm and dragged him indoors. She took him into her little front room, which was hardly ever used, and shaking with rage, she faced the alarmed boy.

'Now you listen to me, Bobby Jones. You go back to your mother, and you tell her something from me. You tell her I know where your father is, see? He's not dead as she's always told you. And he wasn't the great man she's always saying to you, either, and she knows it.'

Bobby went very pale. What was Mrs Pepper saying? His father wasn't dead? But – his mother always said he was!

'My Alf told me about him,' said Mrs Pepper. 'He used to know him. But my Alf made me promise not to say a word to anyone about him, because he was sorry for you and your mother. Alf's a kindly fellow, and wouldn't harm a fly. But you go home now and tell your mother, I'll give her tit for tat, and I'll spread around this village what I know – just like she's been spreading round what she thinks she knows – and doesn't! My Alf isn't in prison, and never will be.'

She took Bobby to the front door and pushed him out. The unhappy, frightened boy stumbled home as fast as he could. What did Mrs Pepper mean? Oh, what did she mean? What was the secret his mother must have been keeping from him so long? His mother was frightened when she saw Bobby's white face. She ran to him and put her arms round him.

'Have those awful boys been after you?' she cried. Bobby pushed her arms away.

'Mum,' he said, 'Mrs Pepper said my father isn't dead. And you've always said he was. She said Mr Pepper knew all about him and had told her – and now that you've set the tale going in the village that Mr Pepper's in prison – which he isn't, anyway – she'll spread round what she knows about *my* father. What is there to know about him?'

Mrs Jones sat down suddenly and gave a groan. She turned her head away from Bobby, who felt more and more frightened and lost in a world of hateful grown-up secrets.

'Mum! You must tell me!' he said in a trembling voice. 'I can't bear not to know now. And anyway – I expect everyone in the village will be able to tell me soon, if you don't. Where *is* my father?'

'Oh, Bobby!' said Mrs Jones in a funny choked voice. 'I never meant to tell you, never. He's – he's in prison! Oh, my poor Bobby, I didn't want you to know. I wanted you to grow up thinking your father was a great man, someone to be proud of. But he wasn't. He was a bad man, a forger, who took a lot of money away from people who couldn't afford to lose any.'

'I – see,' said Bobby, slowly. He couldn't get used to the thought, somehow. He kept saying it over and over in his mind: In prison. My father is in prison. He is a live man, a bad one, instead of a good dead one. In prison. I pitied the Peppers because I thought their father was in prison – but it's mine that is, *mine*!

His mother watched his miserable face and stretched her arms out to him. But he took no notice. He glanced sadly at her.

'Mum, you brought this on us yourself,' he said. 'You put a wrong story round the village – a wicked tale that wasn't true. And now Mrs

Pepper will put a true one round, after holding her tongue all these years. How we shall be laughed at! How can I ever face all the boys again? Why did you set me up to be better than the others? I'm not. Probably I'm worse, because I've got a bad father.'

'Oh, Bobby! Bobby, don't talk like that,' pleaded his mother, wiping her eyes. 'I'll go to Mrs Pepper. I'll beg her to hold her tongue. I'll do anything to make things right for you.'

But Bobby could say no more. He went up to his bedroom, shocked and unhappy; he felt that he could never, never face anyone again.

His mother went hurriedly round to Mrs Pepper's cottage. She saw her in the back garden and called to her.

'Mrs Pepper! Mrs Pepper! Can I have a word with you, please?'

Mrs Pepper saw the anxious, worried look on Mrs Jones's face, and guessed Bobby had already been home. She went indoors and beckoned Mrs Jones to follow. They went into the little front room.

'It isn't any good you begging me to hold my tongue,' said Mrs Pepper roughly. 'You want a lesson, Mrs Jones, and you're going to get it. You've set tittle-tattle going often enough in this village, but this time you've done it once too often, see? My Alf isn't in prison. It's true

199

he borrowed a van and knocked down an old woman – and his mother and me, we were worried and thought he might be sent to prison. But he's been let off. So you have it all wrong!'

'I – I thought I heard you saying he *was* in prison,' said Mrs Jones. 'I'm very, very sorry.'

'It's easy to be sorry now,' said Mrs Pepper. 'The thing is – your man really *is* in prison, because my Alf used to know him, and heard all about him. So why shouldn't I do to you what you tried to do to me?'

'Only because it will hurt my Bobby so much if you tell it all round,' said Mrs Jones, tears welling into her eyes.

'Did you think how it would hurt my children

when you set the tale going about Alf?' demanded Mrs Pepper. 'No, you didn't! You're a mean, spiteful, stuck-up woman, and you're doing your best to bring Bobby up just like you are yourself. He'd be a nice enough lad if you let him mix with the village children and make friends with them, instead of sucking up to the others. Now what'll he feel like? Serves you both right!'

'Please, please don't say anything about Bobby's father,' pleaded Mrs Jones again. 'I'll do anything if only you keep your mouth shut. I'm bitterly ashamed now that I said what I did about Alf. You're a better woman than I am: you knew about my husband and kept the secret for years, but I was spiteful and told tales about you. Can you forgive me, Mrs Pepper?'

'I'll see,' said Mrs Pepper. She was a kind-hearted woman, always generous to both friends and enemies, but she thought it would be very good for Bobby and Mrs Jones to spend a day or two not knowing whether she was going to be kind or not. Let them shiver and shake a little before they found out that she was not going to tell their poor secret.

Maybe they will both learn a little sense then, she thought. Nothing like a bit of suffering to make you understand what others may feel like at times! I shan't say a word about Bobby's father – catch me doing a dirty trick like that, making myself as bad as Mrs Jones! – but they won't know it for a day or two.

'You have a cup of tea and then go back to Bobby,' said Mrs Pepper to Mrs Jones. 'Maybe he'll be needing you. And take my advice, and let him make friends with his own kind. Sucking up to others isn't any good to anybody. Let him make his friends from his own school, that's the best thing for him.'

Mrs Jones went home, still unhappy and ashamed, but a little comforted. If only Mrs Pepper wouldn't tell her secret, how much nicer she would try to be!

20

Sally's Turn
at Last

When she got home Mrs Jones went up to Bobby's bedroom but he wasn't there. She wondered fearfully where he had gone. A wild thought flashed through her mind that he had run away.

But Bobby had not run away. He had sat and thought things over for a while, and then had felt that he could never face the other Put-Em-Rights again. Never. How could he be a Put-Em-Right when his own father was a bad man?

But I can't go and see them and tell them face to face, thought Bobby, feeling sick at the thought of the compassionate faces of the others, I can't. I should break down or something. I'll write them a letter.

So with much thought, one or two tears, and a bad heartache Bobby wrote his letter to the other five Put-Em-Rights. He licked the envelope, slipped out of the house, took a back way so as not to meet any of the village children, and made his way to the Rectory.

He meant to slip the note in the letterbox, but unfortunately he bumped into Amanda who was hurrying back to fetch a trowel. She had begun on the garden at the cottage, only to find there were no tools of any sort there.

'Hello, Bobby!' she said, startled at his miserable face. 'Is anything wrong? Did the Peppers throw anything over you again?'

'When you call a meeting of the Put-Em-Rights again, will you please give this letter to Sally to read out?' said Bobby in such a strange voice that Amanda stared hard at him.

'But – but, Bobby – what's the matter? Why have you written a letter?' cried Amanda, really puzzled and alarmed. 'Oh, don't be so awfully mysterious!'

'I'm sorry, Amanda. I can't tell you anything more now,' said Bobby and he turned his back and walked steadily down the drive. Amanda snatched a trowel and a fork out of the nearby shed and hurried after him.

'Bobby! Do tell me if anything's gone wrong. It's silly to act like this.'

'Don't,' said Bobby, hardly able to keep a steady face when Amanda put her arm round his shoulder. His mouth shook and he could say no more. Amanda walked with him in silence to the gate. Then she gave his arm a quick squeeze and went off to the cottage, where Francie, Micky, Midge and Podge awaited her. They were all helping to weed, except Midge, who contented himself with digging hard every time a bed was cleared. Emily sat in her pram, beautifully clean, gurgling at them all.

Amanda felt Bobby's letter in her pocket. She was very puzzled. Was Bobby going to resign from the Put-Em-Rights? It seemed rather like it. But why?

'I say,' said Amanda to Podge and Micky, in a low voice. 'I just met Bobby, and he looked sort of funny. He gave me a letter for Sally to read out next time we hold a meeting. So I vote we hold one tonight, and see what Bobby's put in his letter.'

'Right,' said Podge. 'I'll bring Yolande over

and Micky can run down and get Sally. I wonder what it's all about.'

They knew at the meeting they held that evening. Amanda handed Bobby's letter to Sally. In a dead silence she slit the envelope and took out the note, which was written in very small and neat handwriting. Sally read it out:

Dear Put-Em-Rights,

This is to tell you I can't possibly belong to the band any longer. I have just found out a very dreadful thing, which I must tell you. Anyway, you'll hear it all round the village very soon, because Mrs Pepper is going to spread the news abroad. My father is a bad man. He was a forger. He is now in prison. You can't imagine how I feel about this. Mum is awfully upset because I know about it, but somehow I can't comfort her and she can't comfort me. So I feel very lonely and miserable. I can't face anyone any more. Please don't come and see me or write to me.

Yours,
Bobby Jones.

Sally read the whole letter out in her steady voice. The others listened in the utmost surprise. Their faces showed their feelings. Yolande's eyes were bright with tears. Micky bit his lip and

looked down at the ground. Amanda stared at Sally with her mouth wide open in surprise. Podge frowned hard. Only Sally looked much as usual. She put down the letter.

'Well!' she said. 'What a bombshell!'

'If it's a bombshell to us, whatever must it have been to Bobby?' said Amanda. 'No wonder he looked so awful when I saw him.'

'Can't we – can't we possibly put things right for him?' said Yolande, her voice quivering. Sally slapped her hand on her knee, and made the others jump.

'Of course! Here is another job for the Put-Em-Rights – under their very noses. My job, this time! I'll put things right in no time!'

'Sally! But how in the world can you?' asked Podge, disbelief in his voice.

'Easy,' answered Sally. 'I'll go down and see Mrs Pepper at once, and insist that she doesn't spread this tale about. Then, once I've got her promise, I can go to Mrs Jones and Bobby, and cheer them up. They can hold up their heads if no one knows about Mr Jones. And I'll make Bobby comfort his mother and his mother comfort Bobby, and probably they'll be closer to one another than they've ever been before.'

Podge felt distinctly doubtful about this extremely sensible and efficient programme. Also he felt a little shocked because Sally had not shown any compassion or sadness for poor old Bobby.

'I don't know, Sally,' he said. 'I'm not sure it would be right for us to interfere in this. You might make a mess of it.'

'Of course I shan't!' said Sally, on her mettle at once. 'I can manage this all right. Leave it to me. It's a real Put-Em-Right job, and it's *my* job, because I'm the only one that hasn't had a turn.'

'Well, go a bit carefully,' said Micky. 'When people are upset they're sometimes a bit touchy, you know. And it isn't everyone that likes to be put right in your way, Sally.'

'What do you mean – my way?' inquired Sally indignantly. 'It's the same way as yours. I think I'd better go straight away now.'

'No, leave it till tomorrow,' said Podge. 'Mrs Pepper's temper may have died down a little by then, and Bobby and his mother will have had a night to sleep over their upset and may feel better. Leave it till tomorrow.'

Sally hated putting anything off, if it had got to be done. But she gave in to Podge. She knew that when he spoke in a certain voice it was better to obey him, or she would find herself in an argument in which she would come off worst. Sally never could keep her temper in an argument and Podge always did.

'All right. I'll go tomorrow, first thing. And then I'll come up here and report. We'll meet at half past ten.'

Sally liked having a job to tackle. She loved arranging and organising. It gave her a sense of power that she enjoyed. She had a quick and clever brain and was often impatient with slower people, whom she thought stupid. She looked forward with pleasure to tackling this latest Put-Em-Right job tomorrow.

I shan't let it hang about for ages, like Micky's job with Midge and Fellin, or make a mess of it like Podge did with the Tupps, she thought. I shall clear it all up straight away. Now – how shall I set about it? What shall I do and say?

Calmly and coolly Sally thought over her task. The matter had to be arranged and finished with, and Sally was going to do it as quickly and smartly as she could. There was not one thought of pity in her heart for Bobby nor did she think of Mrs Jones and her unhappiness at all, except to say firmly to herself that Bobby's mother deserved what had happened.

I shall first of all see Mrs Pepper and tell her what I think, thought Sally, who was never scared of tackling anyone or anything. She could have stood up to a dozen Mr Tupps and beaten them! Then I shall go on and see Mrs Jones, and show her how to get round Bobby. Then I shall find Bobby and tell him he must show extra kindness and love to his mother. So they'll come together again, help one another, and some good will come out of this unhappy muddle.

In this way Sally settled the whole matter in her quick, efficient mind. It was as good as done! Sally thought no more about it when she went to bed that night. If only she had known it, she was the only Put-Em-Right who did not think with discomfort and sadness of Bobby.

Yolande cried into her pillow when she thought of what Bobby must have felt when he heard about his father. She adored her own father. How awful to have a father in prison!

Amanda and Micky said a special prayer for the old Put-Em-Right boy. Amanda thought with love and gratitude of her own father and mother, kind and good, bent always on doing good and helping others.

Podge lay feeling uncomfortable and sorry. He had often jeered at Bobby and tried to take him down a peg. Not that Bobby hadn't deserved it at times (he certainly had), but Podge couldn't help wishing he had been a little more friendly lately. He didn't like Bobby very much, but that was no reason for not being kind when he could. Bobby had so little. Podge had so much.

I could have shared my things a bit more with him, thought Podge. I could have lent him my bike. He did so love riding it. And I could have given him that old stamp album of mine, now I've got two new ones. He would have been thrilled, because he's only got an exercise book to keep his stamps in.

Then Podge thought over the stern words his father had said to him about carelessness and irresponsibility, and he wriggled uncomfortably in bed.

'Dad hasn't got a good opinion of me these hols, and I've got a pretty low one of myself, too. It's odd to set myself up as a Put-Em-Right when there're so many things wrong with myself! I shall have to do something about it. From now on I take care of my things, and show a bit of sense. Dad will soon know I'm a responsible and trustworthy chap if I take myself in hand!'

So the various Put-Em-Rights lay and pondered, falling to sleep one by one. All of them slept well, except Bobby. He lay awake for hours. He thought about his father. Did his mother ever write to him? When was he coming out of prison? Was anyone going to welcome him and help him when he did come out?

Bobby felt certain that his mother would have nothing to do with his father because he had brought disgrace on them. Mum is hard, he thought. She likes to hold her head up and feel she is somebody – and if anyone or anything spoils that, she will hate them and despise them. Mum should have told me about all this. We might even have tried to help my father when he comes out of prison. Oh, I wish I hadn't got to stay here, and have everyone pointing their fingers at me! I shall never be happy again in my life!

21

Miss
Bossy

Sally set off the next morning, full of zeal. She walked to Mrs Pepper's cottage and knocked at the front door. Old Mrs Pepper answered it and looked surprised to see Sally.

'I want to see your daughter, please,' shouted Sally, knowing the old woman was deaf.

'All right, all right. No need to shout at me,' grumbled the old woman, showing Sally into the little front room. 'You've got a sharp enough voice for anyone to hear, without shouting!'

Sally didn't like that remark very much. She knew she had rather a loud, commanding voice, because other people, also disliking it, had pointed it out to her. She sat down firmly on a chair and waited.

She waited and waited. Mrs Pepper was busy finishing her daily washing, for, with so many children, there was always washing to do. She was not going to hurry herself, and waste her precious hot water for 'that little madam of a Sally!'

Sally grew impatient. She tapped her foot on the floor. She was feeling rather cross when Mrs Pepper came at last, her arms still white with soapsuds. 'Well, Sally, this is an early call,' said Mrs Pepper. 'Message from your mother, I suppose? Well, if she wants me to come over and help to cut up the bread and butter for the Women's Outing today, you'll have to tell her I can't. I'm expecting Alf home.'

'I haven't come with a message from my mother,' said Sally. 'I've come upon a much more serious business, Mrs Pepper. Now – you're a Christian woman, aren't you – and you come to church. Well, do you think it is a Christian thing to do, or a kindly thing, to put about that Bobby Jones's father is in prison?'

Mrs Pepper looked at Sally in surprise and dislike. Bossy young miss! Mrs Pepper was not going to 'take any sauce' from people like Sally.

'This is none of your business,' she said curtly to Sally. 'You're not going to tell me what to do or not to do. You mind your own business!'

'This *is* my business,' said Sally firmly. 'You'll be sorry, Mrs Pepper, if you do this thing, and bring shame on Mrs Jones and Bobby. I am sure everyone will think badly of you if you tittle-tattle about such a matter.'

Mrs Pepper never had tittle-tattled. She was a kind and generous-hearted woman who always stopped any unkind talk if she heard it. It made her furious to think that Sally should think she was a tittle-tattler. She went red in the face, and rubbed her hands up and down her soapy arms. She made up her mind to give Sally a shock.

'Now, look here, Miss Bossy,' she said, 'you've come to the wrong house if you think you're going to order someone about. Your mother runs this village, and good luck to her – but you're not going to run it too! One Wilson running this place is quite enough! And let me tell you this, Miss Bossy – I wasn't going to say a word about Bobby's father, not one word, see?

But now you've interfered and tried to boss me round, I've changed my mind! I shall tell every single person what I know about Thomas Jones!'

Sally stared at Mrs Pepper in horror. What, she had never meant to say anything – and now, because of Sally, she was going to spread the news around? Sally sat back and gulped.

'Ah – that makes you think a bit, don't it?' said Mrs Pepper, enjoying Sally's dismay. 'Well, people like you may get quite a lot of things done; but they set as many things going wrong as they try to put right, and all because they put people's backs up, see? You only do things because you're bossy by nature, and you like to have a bit of power and use it. You don't do things like Mrs Gray, the Rector's wife, does -- she does them out of the kindness of her heart and because she wants people to be happy! I'd do anything for her, I would – but not a thing for you!'

'Mrs Pepper – please don't say that,' begged Sally, very much taken aback. 'I didn't mean to be bossy. Don't do anything unkind simply because I put your back up.'

'Well, when you hear everyone talking about Bobby Jones's father being in prison, and pointing their fingers at the poor Joneses, you'll know *you're* to blame for that,' said Mrs Pepper,

who hadn't the remotest idea about saying anything about Mr Jones being in prison, but meant
to frighten and dismay 'Miss Bossy'. 'Now you
go, because I'm busy, what with getting the
children and house clean for Alf to come back
to.'

Sally rose, very downcast. 'Please, Mrs
Pepper,' she began again. But Mrs Pepper
hustled her out of the front door and said good
morning. She smiled to herself as she thought
of Sally's horror at her threat. Serve her right –
sticking her finger into someone else's pie. A bit
of kindness was worth all the bossiness in the
world.

Sally was really horrified. She felt certain Mrs
Pepper meant what she said – and she, Sally,
would be entirely to blame if the tale got about.
The girl hardly knew what to do next. She dared
not go back to the Peppers' again in case she
made Mrs Pepper even more angry.

She smarted under Mrs Pepper's home truths.
How hateful to be called 'Miss Bossy'. She went
slowly along the road, wondering what to do
next. She had so hoped she would be able to
go and tell Mrs Jones and Bobby that everything
was all right, and no one in the village would
hear from Mrs Pepper about Bobby's father.
Now she had messed everything up.

I think perhaps it would be better for the

Joneses to leave this village, thought Sally. Poor Bobby will never get over the boys teasing him about his father, and Mrs Jones will hate it, because she's always been so superior and kept herself to herself. I'd better advise them to leave and then see if Mummy can get Mrs Jones a job somewhere away from here. Bobby can go with her, and start school again without anyone knowing anything.

Having thus decided the Jones's future, Sally felt better. Anxious to set herself right again in her own opinion, she hurried to the Jones's cottage.

Mrs Jones opened the door. Her eyes were red with weeping, and she looked forlorn and miserable. Her misery was not caused by the shock of fearing that Mrs Pepper would spread her secret abroad, but by Bobby's behaviour. The boy had eaten nothing and had kept to his room all the time. He would say nothing to his mother, but hugged his misery to himself. He seemed to have turned completely against her.

Mrs Jones would have welcomed a little kindness from anyone. She felt tired and sad after a sleepless night. She took Sally into her parlour, looking forward to a little warmth and kindness from someone who had been friends with her Bobby. But Sally was so full of her plans that she had no time to show any warm friendliness.

She began to talk in the same efficient tone she used when addressing her form at school.

'Mrs Jones, it must be a great shock to you to know that your secret is no longer a secret. I am sure you must want to get away from here, where people will talk and whisper about you. I believe my mother could get you a job over in Kirklin, where we have relations. If so, you could go there with Bobby and forget about all this.'

Mrs Jones was rather taken aback at this easy disposal of her and Bobby. Why, she might be a bit of furniture the way Sally spoke to her, she thought! She stiffened a little and looked obstinate.

'Thank you,' she said politely, 'but I shall have to think out my own plans. If I want to leave, I have a sister I could go to.'

Sally felt that she had been rebuffed. She wondered if she had been too bossy again. She tried to make her voice kinder, and to think of something nice to say.

'I'm sure Bobby is a great comfort to you,' she said, knowing quite well that he wouldn't be, because of what the boy had said in his letter.

Mrs Jones felt the tears coming into her eyes. She dabbed them away hastily. She did not want to cry in front of Sally.

'I'm worried about Bobby,' she said. 'He

won't eat anything at all. He just shuts himself upstairs and broods. It worries me dreadfully.'

'How selfish and silly of him!' said Sally, who could never understand people not wanting to eat when they were upset. 'He should be doing his best to make up to you for the unhappy life you've had! I'll go up and speak to him. But when he comes down, Mrs Jones, you'll do your bit, won't you, and make a fuss of him and be kind. He's had a great shock.'

'Fancy you telling me to be kind to my own boy!' said Mrs Jones indignantly. Then a suspicion came to her. 'Look here, Sally – are you trying any of that Put-Em-Right stuff on me? Because I won't have it! Impudence, that's what it is, to say nothing of being downright unkind to call my Bobby selfish and silly! You get along home. You've upset me, coming in like this, telling me I'd better leave, and talking against poor Bobby. I thought you were his friend!'

'So I am,' said Sally, surprised at Mrs Jones's outburst, and a little annoyed that she had guessed Sally was being a Put-Em-Right. 'I'm going up to him now.'

Before Mrs Jones could stop her, Sally marched upstairs. She banged on Bobby's door and went in. The boy was lying on his bed, his face to the wall. How feeble! thought Sally. Just like Bobby. He wants pulling together a bit.

So she proceeded to try to pull him together.

'Bobby, how can you lie up here when your poor mother downstairs is quite brokenhearted? You ought not to think of yourself now; you should think of all the years your poor mother has borne this terrible secret.'

'She didn't need to bear it. She could have told me, instead of letting me hear it from an outsider,' said Bobby. 'Anyway, this is none of your business, Sally. You only put me against Mum when you say things like this. I was just feeling I'd go down to her – and now you've spoilt it. I feel hard towards her again. Go away.'

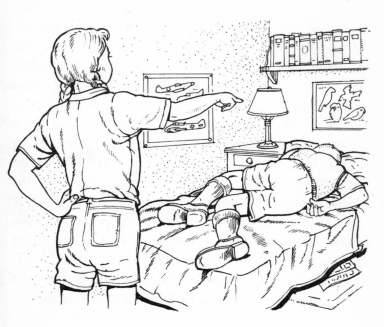

'Oh, Bobby – I didn't mean to – I only meant to – oh, Bobby, do go down,' begged Sally. 'She really will need your help when all the village knows your secret. Mrs Pepper told me this morning she meant to spread it around.'

'You don't mean to say you've been to Mrs Pepper, too?' demanded Bobby, sitting up, red with anger. 'Discussing my affairs with that woman – enjoying yourself a lot, I suppose. Go away, Sally, I hate you!'

'But – but,' began Sally, really taken aback at Bobby's furious voice.

'I said "GO AWAY!"' shouted Bobby, and he leaped off the bed and opened the door. Sally went out, red in the face. Bobby slammed the door so hard that the whole house shook. She did not like to go and see Mrs Jones again, but as she passed the sitting-room Mrs Jones herself came out.

'So you've been upsetting Bobby, too,' she said. 'You keep out of my house in future, Sally Wilson! Not one word of real kindness have you said, not one. Hard as nails you are, just like your mother. I'd rather see that little Yolande than set my eyes on you! She's a kind little thing, timid though she is. But you're afraid of nothing – you just go riding roughshod over everyone's feelings! Real bossy, that's what you are!'

Sally stepped out into the sunshine. She felt

shaken and alarmed. Three people had told her unpleasant things – and yet she had only tried to do her duty, and to make others see their duty, too. Perhaps it wasn't enough to do that. Perhaps there was something more important than to do one's duty to one's neighbour. Perhaps she should just have been kind and understanding? With her face burning, Sally walked away, not seeing Mrs Pepper passing her on her way to the village.

But Mrs Pepper saw Sally. 'She's been in to the Joneses!' said Mrs Pepper to herself. 'Interfering little miss! Been to tell them I said I'd set the tale round, I suppose – made them thoroughly frightened and miserable. What a girl! I'd box the ears of any of mine that ran round putting people right like Sally!'

She stopped outside the Jones's house. Should she go in and tell Mrs Jones not to worry, she didn't mean to spread the secret round, she'd only said that to shock Sally? Yes – she would! Mrs Jones had had her lesson – now a bit of kindness wouldn't do any harm!

22

Mrs Pepper puts Things Right

Mrs Pepper went briskly in at the gate. She rang the bell. Mrs Jones opened the door, hoping her eyes didn't look too red. She was rather taken aback at the sight of her visitor.

'I'm coming in for a minute,' said Mrs Pepper, and in she went, and through to the sitting-room. 'Poor thing, you look washed out. Now, look here, I haven't come to upset you, I've only come to say that of course I'm not going to breathe a word about your husband. Not a word. I just said that to you in the heat of the moment, and I told that interfering Sally I was going to, too, to give her a shock, the bossy little creature!'

'Oh,' said Mrs Jones, her face growing lighter. 'Oh! Do you really mean – you're not going to say a word to anyone? No one will know?'

'Not a soul,' said Mrs Pepper. 'I'm not one to gossip round, never have been, and I'm not going to start now. You were wrong to do what you did, and maybe you'll have learned a lesson now, and won't gossip again yourself. I'm sorry for you, Mrs Jones – it must be hard to have your man in prison, and hard for your boy to know it too.'

Mrs Jones felt the tears coming to her eyes again and she hastily dabbed them away. 'Yes,' she said, 'it's been hard, but I hoped Bobby would never know, and maybe I could bring him up to be better than his father was – and so be proud of my son, if I couldn't be proud of his father.'

'Well, it seems to me you're going the wrong way about it,' said sensible Mrs Pepper. 'Filling his head with all kinds of grand ideas, instead of letting him make friends with the children he knows. You let him come to tea with my twins sometimes; they'll be good for him! And he'll be good for them, too, for he's got nice manners, your Bobby has. I've always said he was a nice boy if it wasn't that he sucked up to children who probably didn't want him!'

The real kindness in Mrs Pepper's voice, and the common sense in her words, warmed Mrs Jones. She began to feel almost happy. She needn't leave the village! She could still hold up her head. No one would point their fingers at Bobby. Things suddenly seemed very much brighter.

'You've done me good,' she said to Mrs

Pepper. 'That Sally properly upset me.'

For a few minutes the two talked vigorously about Sally and her failings. Then Mrs Jones put the kettle on to make a cup of tea for herself and Mrs Pepper. She found herself liking the sensible woman immensely. How could she have been so silly as to hold herself aloof from everyone, and look down on them? Why, Mrs Pepper was a far better person than she was!

Mrs Pepper went to the bottom of the stairs and called up to Bobby.

'Hey, Bobby, come on down and have a cup of tea and a biscuit! I've just popped in with some good news for your mother.'

Bobby, astonished and hopeful, appeared downstairs. One glance at his mother's face and he knew things were all right. He didn't know how they were all right, but they were, and that was all that mattered. To his mother's delight, he ate half a plateful of biscuits and answered Mrs Pepper's cheerful questions quite politely. Mrs Pepper went away leaving behind her a very warm and cheerful feeling. 'She's not going to tell a soul,' said Mrs Jones happily. 'Not a soul – and she means it, Bobby. I'm glad you know all about things, dear – it's a help somehow. I ought to have told you before.'

'Yes, you ought, Mum,' said Bobby, and he got up to kiss his mother. 'I'm old enough to share things with you now, you know I am. We'll plan the future together. You tell me all about my father – and when he's coming out of prison – and if there's any chance of helping him, and keeping him right – and everything. It's been a shock, but I'm all right now. There's one thing – the Put-Em-Rights won't have anything more to do with me, I'm sure of that! So I'll do what I should have done before – I'll make friends with the village children and enjoy the kind of life they live, instead of hanging on to the others, sucking up and pretending all the time!'

This was the longest speech Bobby had ever made in his life, and the most sensible. Mrs Jones gave him a hug. They felt very close together.

Just then someone came up the path and Bobby gave an exclamation. 'It's Yolande! What does she want?'

He opened the door. Yolande smiled at him. She held out something and said, 'Bobby, I've brought you that pencil of mine you liked so much the other day, and please I'm very sorry about what you said in your letter, but of course it doesn't make any difference at all. You're my friend just the same.'

The little bit of real kindness touched both Bobby and Mrs Jones. How like Yolande that was! She had been scared to come, but she had come, impelled by her own kind little heart. She would not stay, but scuttled away like a frightened rabbit.

Then Podge and Micky came together, Podge with his old stamp album for Bobby, and Micky with a bag of humbugs, Bobby's favourite sweets. Poor Micky had once more delved into his fast-emptying money-box!

The boys brought a kind little note from Amanda, who had as usual hurried off to the cottage to finish the garden. All the Put-Em-Rights except Sally had come to Bobby, or sent to him, with kindness and friendliness. It seemed to Bobby that, far from disliking him, they liked him even better now! The little kindnesses warmed his heart and took away the last of his unhappiness. He beamed at Podge and Micky.

'Oh, thanks. You *are* kind! And please thank Amanda, too.'

'Can you come to tea this afternoon?' asked Micky. 'It's a little celebration. I'm buying Midge from Fellin!'

'*Buying him!*' said Bobby in surprise. 'Whatever do you mean?'

'Well,' said Micky, 'I've done all I can to make Fellin kinder to Midge, as you know – but last night I caught him thrashing him dreadfully, goodness knows why. Fellin said something about going after a sheep, but I bet Midge

wouldn't go after an enormous sheep. He'd be too frightened. So I told Fellin what I thought of him.'

'Did you really? What did he say?' said Bobby with great interest. 'How brave of you!'

'Fellin said, "If you're so fond of the dog as you seem, you'd better buy him from me! But as long as he's my dog, I shall whip him every day if I like!"'

'So you bought him!' said Bobby. 'How much did you have to pay?'

'Ten pounds,' said Micky with a sigh. 'There's practically nothing in my money-box now. But I don't mind as much as I thought I would – because Midge really is a lovely little dog now, and very good company. The only thing is that when I go back to school, Mum will have to look after him; she's already got so much to do, I don't like to ask her to do any more.'

'Anyway – we're having a celebration tea for Midge, so will you come?' said Podge. Bobby nodded. Yes – he would come just once more, he thought. But after that he would break away from these kind children, and make friends in his own school.

Sally came to tea, too – a very much subdued Sally, who did not look at Bobby, and hardly spoke to him. The boy ignored her, for he felt that of all his friends she had been the one to hurt him, and the one who had showed him no kindness.

Sally had heard of the others' small presents and kindnesses to Bobby, and she was ashamed of herself. Why hadn't she thought of something like that herself? She had been far too bossy and not nearly kind enough. She remembered what the headmistress of her school had said in her report, and for the first time she saw the truth of the words.

Kindness is the one thing that really matters, thought Sally. I must remember that. I'm too quick and hard and I drive others instead of trying to guide them. I must be kinder. I absolutely and completely failed in my Put-Em-Right job. I shall have to tell the others sometime, I suppose – if Bobby hasn't told them already!

Bobby hadn't. He was loyal to Sally, though he disliked her. He left just after tea, and the five Put-Em-Rights played with Midge.

'I say,' said Sally suddenly, 'I expect you are all wanting to know how I got on with my Put-Em-Right job. I guess you saw by Bobby's behaviour to me that I – that I had failed.'

'Yes. We guessed that,' said Podge, rather gravely. 'What happened?'

Sally, who was a truthful girl, told the Put-Em-Rights everything, and did not spare herself. She wanted to get it off her chest, then put it behind her and start all over again. The other four listened in silence. They all thought the same: Sally's hard. She doesn't know what it is to be kind.

'Well, there you are,' said Sally, finishing her tale. 'I failed with Mrs Pepper. I failed with Mrs Jones and Bobby. I put them all against me. Bobby's told you that Mrs Pepper isn't going to say anything after all – but that wasn't my doing! I caused her to say she was going to be as spiteful as she could be. I was so relieved to hear she had changed her mind.'

'You certainly failed completely,' said Podge. 'But actually I don't think this was a job for us to do. We shouldn't have let you try. Anyway, I knew you'd be too bossy. You'll have to stop that bossiness of yours, Sally, or you'll put everyone against you as you grow up.'

'I know,' said Sally humbly. 'I'm going to try, Podge. I feel awful about this. Please believe me. I'm not fit to be a Put-Em-Right really, I suppose. I ought to put myself right first!'

'Perhaps we all ought to,' said Podge. 'I've felt a bit awful lately, too – thinking that that trouble with the Tupps really blew up because I was careless enough to leave my bike out. That's worried me quite a bit. My father ticked me off properly for that.'

'And although I've done my job in the cottage

with Francie, and you've all praised me, I feel rather bad too,' confessed Amanda.

'But why?' said Podge in surprise. 'You and Yolande did really well.'

'Yes – I've worked like a slave in that cottage, but really only to show Francie I wasn't lazy, as she said I was,' said Amanda. 'But I never do a thing for Mummy, do I? That's how I ought to put myself right, I think, and that's what I'm going to do, as soon as I've done this job. I'm going to take on a lot of things for Mummy.'

'Good for you, Amanda!' said Podge approvingly. 'Jolly good.'

'We shan't be able to meet again for a little while,' said Micky. 'Amanda and I have got two cousins coming, and we'll have to entertain them. We'll meet again when they've gone.'

'And Yo's got her mother and father back for a week or two, and ought to stay with them,' said Podge. 'And I've told Dad I'll do a bit of extra work now – I had a bad report last term. So the Put-Em-Rights had better part for a while, and then meet later on in the hols. Anyway, we've all had a turn and done our bit, haven't we?'

'Some better than others,' said Sally a little bitterly.

'Cheer up, Sally,' said Podge. 'Why don't you ask Mandy's mother if you can help her in her parish jobs a little? If Mandy helps in the house, and you help in the parish, Mrs Gray will have quite a holiday! She looks as if she wants one. She's so kind – you can learn a bit from her – that is, if you really do want to!'

Sally did want to. She was clever enough to know she had been stupid, and now that she realised that a little warmth and kindness would get many things put right far more quickly than bossiness or efficiency, she wanted to change herself a bit. Two of Sally's best points were her ability to see herself clearly after a mistake, and her honesty in trying to set things right.

'I'll go and talk to Mrs Gray now,' she said, getting up. 'No time like the present!'

'Good old Sally – as quick off the mark as ever!' said Podge. 'I must say she's a lot nicer when she's been a failure than when she's been a success!'

23

Rene
comes Home

For the next week or two the six Put-Em-Rights did not see as much of one another as before. Micky and Amanda were busy with their two small cousins. Yolande was with her father and mother, and Podge was doing his best to get back into his father's good books.

Sally was a great surprise to Mrs Gray. Each day the girl came up to the Rectory and asked quite humbly if she might help the Rector's wife in her parish work.

'Well – what do you want to do, Sally?' Mrs Gray asked kindly, not at first quite liking the idea of having the rather dictatorial girl around.

'Anything, Mrs Gray, from doing the flowers in the church for you, to taking round parish notices and magazines,' replied Sally earnestly. 'And – well – if I could just come round with you sometimes, when you visit people who are ill or in trouble, I'd be very glad.'

After a day or two Mrs Gray was delighted with Sally. It was quite plain that the girl really wanted to help – and to help in the right way. Almost gone were Sally's quick, commanding tones and bossy little ways. She was so much gentler and kinder that Mrs Gray and the Rector marvelled, wondering what in the world could have changed Sally so completely.

'And there's Amanda, too – she's puzzled me this last week,' said Mrs Gray to the Rector. 'Always offering to do this and that for me in the house – and yesterday, when she found me polishing those bookcases of yours, my dear, she actually took the duster and polish out of my hand, and finished the job herself. She did it as well as I could have done it.'

'I'm glad,' said the Rector. 'It has always saddened me that Amanda should be so lazy and selfish, and that Micky should be so mean. But even Micky seems to have changed, too, lately!'

'Yes – his money-box is quite empty,' said Mrs Gray. 'Well, he spent a lot on little Midge, you know, buying the collar and then buying Midge from Fellin! I've been rather proud of him, because I know Micky doesn't find it as easy as Amanda to be generous.'

'Where did Amanda go rushing about to the last week or so?' asked the Rector. 'I so often met her tearing down to the village.'

'Oh, she went to Mrs Potts's cottage and helped to get it clean, with Francie, Mrs Potts's

sister,' explained Mrs Gray. 'We ought to walk down there today and look in, because Rene Potts comes back from hospital, and I believe Ted is expected home any time. We'll take Rene some flowers, shall we?'

So that afternoon Mrs Gray and the Rector walked down to Rene Potts's little cottage. To their surprise, Amanda was there, too, with Francie, and baby Emily. Both girls were in a great state of excitement. The cottage was spick and span. Everything was clean and spotless. The kettle shone as it boiled on the stove. The curtains were snowy. The sink was shining.

The garden was a picture – and in the middle of it was Ted's rose-tree, with a number of beautiful red roses on it. The little path was free from weeds. The gate no longer hung crooked for Podge had mended it. The baby was dressed in the clothes that Podge's mother had given him two or three weeks back. She had rosy cheeks now, and looked very beautiful with her black curls and big eyes. She crowed for joy when she saw so many people.

'Mummy! I didn't know you and Daddy were coming this afternoon!' Amanda cried joyfully. 'Mummy, this is Francie, Rene Potts's sister. We both did the cottage and garden together, to get it ready for when Rene and her husband came back. We're expecting Rene any minute now. Do you think the cottage looks nice? And look at Emily!'

Mrs Gray was almost too amazed to speak. She knew how dirty and untidy both cottage and garden had been, and she had herself tried to get Rene to take more interest in the baby: now here were all three looking beautiful. She beamed at the shy Francie and the excited Amanda.

'Well, you two girls *have* done well! It's a splendid job, and I never saw such a change in any baby. Rene will be pleased!'

'Here she comes! Someone's bringing her

home in their car!' cried Amanda, and sure enough a small car drove up to the tiny gate, and out got Rene, looking rather pale, but very pretty.

She stood and stared when she saw the tidy garden full of flowers, with the rose-tree blossoming in the middle. She stared when she saw how beautiful Emily looked. She stared when she saw the clean and tidy little cottage!

'Oh!' she said, with a gulp. 'I never knew home could look so sweet! Emily! Do you remember your mum?' She flung herself on the surprised baby and took her out of her pram, her eyes brimming with happy tears.

'Isn't she a love? Oh, she looks so beautiful! Kiss Mummy, Emily!'

Everybody had a lump in their throats when they saw Rene's delight and pleasure. It had been worth all the hard work, thought Amanda and Francie. It really had.

'Come and have a cup of tea, Rene,' said Francie, 'I've got the kettle on. And Ma baked a cake for you, special. It's a ginger one, the kind you like.'

Mrs Gray gave Rene the flowers she had brought, and the Rector said a few kind words. 'Coming back to tea, Amanda?' he said to his small daughter.

'Well, I'd like to have it with Rene and Francie

really,' said Amanda, who was longing to see Rene's surprise at everything in the clean little cottage. 'Francie asked me to stay.'

'Very well,' said Mrs Gray, smiling, and she and Amanda's father walked home. Amanda hopped into the cottage. Rene's surprise and pleasure were deep and genuine. She found it difficult to believe that Francie and Amanda had done so much. Why, it was like a new place!

'It's good to be home,' she said, as they all sat round the table eating cake and drinking their tea. 'Especially when everything's so perfect, and Emily looking so bonny. I'm much better now. I'll be able to keep things going myself – and you'll see I'll keep this place just as beautiful as you've got it! If only Ted was here to see it all!'

It wasn't more than two minutes after she had said that, that Rene gave a squeal which made the two girls and Emily jump almost out of their skins. Rene was pointing out of the window with a trembling finger.

'Look! Oh, look! Isn't that Ted himself?'

It was! A very brown, tall, lean Ted, dressed in a sailor's uniform, a bag on his strong shoulders. He stopped at the little gate and looked with pride and joy at his house and garden, both so trim and neat. He saw the rose-tree in the middle full of red roses. He walked in, went to

the rose-tree and picked the biggest red rose
there.

Then he went to the open door of the cottage
to find Rene. She was there to meet him, her
face radiant. What a day, what a wonderful day!
She had got back her home, her baby and her
husband all at once, and she looked lovely with
happiness.

'Come on. Let's go,' said Francie, in a low
voice. 'They'll not want us hanging around here.

We'll slip out of the back door. Come on, Amanda!'

Amanda, her eyes taking in the happiness of the two people, seeing Ted give his wife the red rose to show he loved her, hearing Emily crow with delight to see yet another visitor, was quite lost. She sat there, staring, and Francie had to give her a sharp nudge.

'Come on, Amanda, I tell you! They don't want us. We've done our bit, and we must go.'

'Yes,' said Amanda, sighing, and got up to go. The two girls slipped out of the back door and went across the field there. They looked at one another.

'That was a wonderful surprise for Rene,' said Francie. 'Won't my ma be pleased to hear it when I tell her! She was going over to see Rene this evening, and I guess she'll hurry as fast as her legs will take her. What a bit of news!'

'It was lovely,' said Amanda. 'Oh, Francie, I *am* glad we worked so hard. But I really enjoyed it, didn't you?'

'It was fun having you there,' said Francie. 'I wouldn't have done a thing by myself. It was nice to see Rene's face when she got home!'

The girls parted and Amanda shot off to the Rectory to tell the news of Ted's sudden homecoming at the exact right moment. Everyone was thrilled.

'Mandy, I feel rather proud of you,' said her mother. 'I didn't realise at first that it was you and Francie alone who made such a difference to that cottage and garden – and to that dear little baby, too. You must have worked very hard.'

'We did, rather,' said Amanda. 'The boys helped in the garden, too. Yo helped sometimes as well. It was quite fun. I learned an awful lot, Mummy. Francie laughed at me sometimes because I didn't do things right. But now I know how to.'

'Dr Paget to see you,' said Alice, the daily help, coming in suddenly. 'Podge is here, too, and Yolande.'

'Oh – news about Will, I expect!' cried Micky. 'Hello, Podge; hello, Yo!'

It was news about Will – and very good news too. Dr Paget had watched him for some days and had soon made up his mind that Will could be helped.

'So Will will be quite all right soon!' cried Yolande. 'He'll never have that silly habit of wanting to steal everything bright that he sees. He'll not be stupid any more. He'll be a good, ordinary boy!'

'Well, that certainly is good news!' said the Rector, delighted. 'Have you told Mrs Tupp?'

'Yes, we've just been there with the good

news,' said Podge. 'You should have seen poor Mrs Tupp! She didn't know whether to laugh or cry, so she did both. And she kissed Uncle's hands. He went so red!'

'Well, I'm not used to having my hands kissed!' said Dr Paget. 'Poor woman, she was overjoyed, and I don't wonder. The man was intensely grateful too. He'll be one of your father's best farmhands, Podge.'

'It's funny to think how bitter and angry he was, that time I went to see him!' said Podge. 'I was scared stiff!'

'Not nearly as scared as I was – I ran like a hare!' said Yolande, remembering.

'Well, you children certainly seem to have been taking plenty of people's affairs into your own hands,' said the Rector, amazed. 'I think I shall resign and let you carry on with the work of the parish!'

24

The Last Meeting of the Put-Em-Rights

A few days after that, the Put-Em-Rights held their last meeting during those holidays. Bobby's school was beginning again, and so was Sally's. Micky, Amanda, Podge and Yolande were going to the sea together for a week before their schools began.

'So this will have to be the last meeting,' said Podge as they all sat down in the field outside the Rectory garden.

'It's been fun to be the Put-Em-Rights,' said Amanda. 'I don't know that we have been awfully successful really – except with Will Tupp – but I suppose it hasn't been a waste of time.'

'No, it certainly hasn't,' said Sally in such a serious voice that they all looked hard at her. 'We've all learned a lot of things ourselves – things that will help us to help other people much more than we ever could before. Take me – I never realised before what an awfully bossy person I was! Now I know, and I'm going to be careful in future.'

'Oh, Sally, you're quite a different person already!' cried Amanda warmly. 'I know, because I heard Mummy say to Daddy yesterday that she never knew before what a kind heart you had, and she said what a help you had been to her! And anyway we can see ourselves that you're different. You don't order us around so much, and even your voice is different. It's softer and warmer, somehow – more like my mother's.'

Sally was pleased, and in her turn she praised Amanda. Indeed, everyone felt that they had a word of praise for the once lazy and selfish little girl.

'You're a real help to your mother now,' said Sally. 'She told me so yesterday. She said she didn't know what she'd do without you, when you went back to school. You must have learned a lot, working with Francie!'

'I did,' said Amanda. 'I suppose we've all learned something, really. Podge isn't careless or silly any more! He hasn't lost a thing for weeks!'

'I've grown up a bit,' said Podge, with a laugh. 'Time I did too. I could be head of my form if I worked hard enough, and I mean to, now. My word, Dad will get a shock – but a pleasant one – when he sees my report next term!'

'I suppose I'm the only one that hasn't learned anything really,' said Yolande, but the others pooh-poohed this idea at once.

'Why, Yo, you're not afraid of things any more!' said Podge. 'You're as brave as can be! You didn't even mind giving out the prizes at the Baby Show yesterday!'

'Well, I got awfully excited when I saw that it was Emily who had won first prize,' said Yolande. 'That was lovely. And now I come to think of it I didn't feel scared at having to stand up in public and give out prizes. So I suppose I must have learned to be a bit braver. But not very much, really.'

'Well, you've made a start, Yo, and that's what matters!' said Podge encouragingly.

'What has old Mick learned?' asked Amanda, looking at her brother with bright eyes. She knew better than anyone what he had learned.

'Nothing,' said Micky gloomily. 'I failed in my job – didn't make any change in old Fellin, though I did in Midge. But it's easy to change a dog, if you're kind to him. The funny thing is, even though he's my dog now, and I'm always kind to him, and Fellin never was, he often wanders back to Fellin's cottage to see him!'

'Bad taste on his part,' said Podge. Amanda interrupted him.

'I know what old Micky's learned!' she said,

putting a hand on his shoulder. 'And I'm going to say it, because he ought to get a word of praise, too. He's learned to be generous! You have, Mick, it's no use denying it. You don't hang on to your money like a miser, as you used to do. You hand it out quite cheerfully, and this week you gave me the very nicest birthday present I've ever had from you.'

'Good old Mick,' said Podge approvingly. 'He certainly deserves his word of praise, too. He was jolly patient with Fellin and Midge – but Fellin was too hard a nut for anyone to crack!'

All this time Bobby had sat and said nothing.

He had never been one to say very much, anyhow, except to agree with the others, but lately he had been even more silent. He had looked quite happy, but he seemed serious and determined.

He knew the lesson he had learned, and he was not going to forget it – but he didn't want to talk about it. However, he was saved from any awkward explanations by Sally.

'I think we'd really better bring the Put-Em-Rights to an end,' she said seriously. 'We did do some good; but we did far more good to ourselves, I think, than to other people – still, on the whole, I think we all agree it's not so easy for children to put the world right as they think! We've tried very hard, but now we'd better stop. Perhaps next hols we could think of something else instead.'

'I agree with Sally,' said Podge. 'I think we'd better end the Put-Em-Rights, too. We had some excitement and it was awfully interesting, and it taught us a lot. Anyway, we're all going back to school soon, so we'll have to drop it during term time.'

Everyone agreed, Bobby more heartily than anyone. It would be easy to drop out of the little circle of friends when the next holidays came. The others wouldn't really miss him, he knew that.

'There's only one thing I wish,' said Micky, lying back on the grass. 'I do wish I'd had more success with my job. It's been a great disappointment to me that Fellin was so hard and cruel, and that I couldn't change him. And now the snag is, I'll have to go back to school soon, and leave Midge behind for Mum to look after. And I really don't want to give her any more jobs to do.'

The others considered this. Bobby wondered if he should ask his mother whether he could look after Midge. But she didn't like dogs, and anyway Bobby wanted to break completely with these friends of his now. It would be the easiest way. So he said nothing.

Then there came an interruption to the discussion. Alice, the daily help, called over the hedge.

'Micky! Fellin wants to see you a minute. Can you come?'

Micky sat up, surprised. 'Wonder what he wants?' he said. 'Oh, dear, I hope he hasn't come to complain that Midge has been down to his cottage and has chased one of his hens or something!'

Everyone got up to go with Micky, curious to know what Fellin wanted.

He was standing on the garden path, Midge at his heels, wagging his tail – an unusual sight to see, for Midge's tail was usually down when he was anywhere near Fellin.

Micky went over to Fellin. 'Did you want to see me?' he asked.

'Yes, Micky,' said Fellin, looking rather awkward. 'I've come to say – would you let me buy this here dog back again?'

Micky was too astonished to speak. Fellin looked still more uncomfortable. 'I know you think I've been cruel to him, and so I have, and I was glad to sell him to you and get rid of him. But he keeps coming and scratching at my door, and seems to want me, somehow. So yesterday I let him in, and he ran round wagging his tail nineteen to the dozen, acting right pleased to be in my room again.'

'I see,' said Micky. 'So you want him for your own again? I don't think I can let him go, though, Mr Fellin. He's happy here with me. He loves a pat, a good dinner, a walk, and a kind word. You would only whip him again when you lost your temper.'

'See here, I promise never to touch him again!' said Fellin, twisting his cap round and round in his hands. 'I've watched you with him, Micky, and I've seen how you changed him into a grand dog. I always wanted a dog for company, see, and now that Midge seems to want me and comes round to my cottage, well, I want him too. I'll feed him well and treat him well, I promise you that.'

'Yes, but do you like him?' asked Micky anxiously. 'I'm not letting Midge go unless you really do like him.'

'I feel as if he's my dog,' said Fellin, and that decided it. If Fellin felt like that, perhaps Midge would be all right.

'Well, you can have him then,' said Micky.

Fellin put his hand in his pocket, and pulled out some money. 'Here's the ten pounds you gave me for him,' he said, 'and how much did you say that collar was, Micky?'

'You can keep the money if you promise to be kind to Midge,' said Micky. But Fellin wouldn't keep the money.

'I shan't feel as if he's my dog unless I pays you back for him,' he said.

'Well, all right then,' said Micky. 'But don't pay me for the collar. Midge can have that as a present from me because he's a nice little dog.'

Fellin paid Micky and then he and Midge went off together, Fellin's surly face looking quite bright. Midge trotted at his heels, wagging his tail.

The others fell on Micky in delight.

'Mick! Your Put-Em-Right job was the biggest success of all! You changed Fellin because you changed Midge! Who would have thought it? Micky, aren't you proud?'

Micky was. His face shone. He rattled the money in his pocket.

'I vote we all go down to the village shop and have ice creams and lemonade,' he said. 'I feel rich. Look at all my money! And now I'll have enough, too, to buy Dad a nice birthday present. What a bit of luck!'

Off they went, talking happily. What a nice ending to the Put-Em-Rights!

They sat down to their ice creams and lemonade. They filled their glasses and drank.

'Here's to the Put-Em-Rights all over the

world!' said Podge. 'Good luck to them, whoever they are, and wherever they live. Here's to
everyone who tries to put things right!'

'To the Put-Em-Rights!' shouted the others,
and down went the ice-cold lemonade. 'To the
Put-Em-Rights all over the world!'